ARMY OF THE DAMNED

The flames grew, consuming a steady stream of bodies. Twin trails of white-shirts snaked out of the ruins, carrying corpses large and small for cremation.

"Look down there," Charlie said, pointing upstream.

A line of white-shirts stood at the edge of the water, the one nearest the edge stretching his arms toward the south bank. Radiation damage had caused the bones in his skull to collapse like an overripe melon.

Suddenly the once-human creature lurched forward into the water. He flapped his arms for a few seconds and then was dragged under by the current. Soon he joined the legion of drowned bodies bobbing in the stream.

"Lemmings," Donovan muttered with disgust and loathing. He had thought he ended the white-shirts' reign of terror in the battle for San Francisco. He was wrong.

*Other Thrilling Adventures
in the **OMEGA SUB** Series
from Avon Books*

(#1) OMEGA SUB
(#2) COMMAND DECISION

Coming Soon

(#4) BLOOD TIDE

Avon Books are available at special quantity discounts for bulk purchases for sales promotions, premiums, fund raising or educational use. Special books, or book excerpts, can also be created to fit specific needs.

For details write or telephone the office of the Director of Special Markets, Avon Books, Dept. FP, 1350 Avenue of the Americas, New York, New York 10019.

CITY OF FEAR

J.D. CAMERON

AVON BOOKS • NEW YORK

If you purchased this book without a cover, you should be aware that this book is stolen property. It was reported as "unsold and destroyed" to the publisher, and neither the author nor the publisher has received any payment for this "stripped book."

OMEGA SUB #3: CITY OF FEAR is an original publication of Avon Books. This work has never before appeared in book form. This work is a novel. Any similarity to actual persons or events is purely coincidental.

AVON BOOKS
A division of
The Hearst Corporation
1350 Avenue of the Americas
New York, New York 10019

Copyright © 1991 by Michael Jahn
Published by arrangement with the author
Library of Congress Catalog Card Number: 91-91770
ISBN: 0-380-76050-9

All rights reserved, which includes the right to reproduce this book or portions thereof in any form whatsoever except as provided by the U.S. Copyright Law. For information address Siegel & Siegel, Ltd., P.O. Box 20304, Dag Hammarskjold Postal Center, New York, New York 10017.

First Avon Books Printing: July 1991

AVON TRADEMARK REG. U.S. PAT. OFF. AND IN OTHER COUNTRIES, MARCA REGISTRADA, HECHO EN U.S.A.

Printed in the U.S.A.

RA 10 9 8 7 6 5 4 3 2 1

For Ellen Jahn

1

The majestic submarine moved steadily through the warm South Pacific seas, tense, like a jungle cat silently stalking her prey.

The sea was shallow, only a few thousand fathoms, but the rim of the deep sea trench lay only ten miles away to starboard, slightly off the bow. Beyond it the ocean plunged swiftly to a depth of nearly three miles. To port and also off the bow, at the distance of seven miles, was the first rising of a coral atoll. The old volcanic mountain rose quickly from the seafloor and swept up above the clear blue surface, where it had been eroded by ten million years of waves and monsoons. Now it was just the hollow of a coral atoll that had been ground down and left deserted by thermonuclear pounding during the fifth decade of the last century.

It was still radioactive, but in a curious way. It was a radioactive antique, with quaint waveform patterns that immediately identified it as a relic of mid-twentieth-century nuclear testing. The testing had gone into making the nuclear weapons that, nine years after the turn of the century, destroyed the known world.

Donovan peered at the atoll on the bridge display. Fashioned from the electrons of LCD wizardry, it showed as a gray-green icon in the shape of a reedlike volcano, only the very tip of which was out of the water. Beside the shimmering icon, a set of numbers showed the residual radiation.

"Those numbers are straight out of the history books," said Alexandra Fisher, who was settling into the role of the science specialist rather well, considering she had only been aboard the submarine for three months and was the only female officer.

"Yeah. I never thought I'd get nostalgic about antique radiation figures," Donovan agreed. The captain rested his hand lightly on the shoulder of his science specialist, who was also his lover.

"This island was smacked by thermonuclear blasts for six straight years. The dose of radiation it got will be with it for ten thousand more years. It will live on as a monument to the heyday of atmospheric nuclear testing."

"Are we safe near it?"

"Safe enough," Alex said. "The hull can shield us from ten times the radiation."

"Then it would make a good place for a sub like us to hide."

Several sets of eyebrows arched when the captain said that. There was, to the best of everyone's knowledge, no other sub like theirs. The U.S.S. *Liberator* was a new boat, the prototype of the new Omega class of nuclear-powered tactical submarines built to usher in the millennium.

Liberator started her design life as an advance on the San Diego–class submarine, with an added forty feet in length for a total of 400 LOA. The extra beam of thirty-seven feet allowed the ship to carry forty Mark 70 long-range, laser-guided, acoustic-homing torpedoes with a range of 25,000 yards; twenty-four Mark 97N antiship missiles with field-grade nuclear warheads and a 250-mile range; and the experimental weapon that was conceivably the biggest advance in submarine warfare in decades, the blue-green laser.

The laser was an outgrowth of technology originally designed for surface-to-sub communications. Never before tested in battle, the weapons were fired from turrets mounted fore and aft on the tower. They could fire up to strike the hulls of surface targets or down to hit submerged targets. The range of effectiveness as a weapon was only 1,000 yards and the damage it could cause was mainly the disruption of electrical circuits, but that was damaging enough to a submarine, and the accuracy was pinpoint. And at longer ranges, up to 10,000 yards, the laser worked as an information probe. When tied into the *Liberator*'s Cyclops information-display system, the laser provided pinpoint accuracy on the location of items ranging from other ships to floating debris and even to thermoclines.

Everything aboard ship was named by the men and with logic in mind. The engines not only were called simply "the engines," they were located in the engine room, which was reached by walking down the engine room corridor. The same went for the reactors, and there was no other place to find the torpedoes but in the torpedo room. The front of the boat was the bow and the back was the stern. There was no conning tower to speak of, only a hydrodynamic blister that was planned as a topsides extension of the bridge. It was called, simply, "the bridge," and it was assumed that the men were smart enough to realize that, when the ship was submerged, the captain meant that part of it inside the main hull. Throughout *Liberator*, practice was to call things by the names that the men were most likely to use. Few confusing post–World War Two Navy acronyms had survived into the age of *Liberator*.

The exception was Cyclops, the tactical eyes and ears of *Liberator*. A marvel of advanced electronic and holographic technology, it took information from the sub's sensors, primarily sonar when under water but including radar, UHF and satellite information when surfaced, and used it to construct a three-dimensional image of the ship and its environment. The name was derived from Cycle Optics, the idea being that Cyclops presented a visual reconstruction of entire cycles of data available on course, the condition of the sea, subsea terrain, and surface threats—ranging from icebergs to flotsam. Cyclops used mainly sonar images, but enhanced them with whatever information was available, and then some. The operator could even plug in the captain's intuition; if Donovan thought that an enemy submarine was hiding behind a nearby seamount, that intuition could be displayed on Cyclops. The operator—and the rest of the bridge crew—would see a three-dimensional visualization of seamount and enemy submarine and the *Liberator*'s position in relation to them, all displayed in shimmery blue and green light that hovered in front of and partly surrounded the helmsman and captain, rather like the heads-up display of a fighter plane. In battle, Donovan could remain at his station, watch the Cyclops visuals, and guide the *Liberator* through the hazards. In peace and in an interesting subsea terrain, he could take the helm just to enjoy the view. In that way *Liberator* could fulfil both her missions—as warship and as research vessel, studying and recording the life of the sea while preparing for the defense of the nation.

Liberator's main advance over the San Diego–class submarines that preceded her lay in the extent to which she was automated. Shipboard systems and procedures that once took three shifts of three or four men each were computerized, roboticized, and manageable by one man per shift. Instead of 120 or more men, *Liberator* was manned by 45 men working in three shifts of 15 each. There was a large computer and systems repair crew to ensure that the automated systems kept running well, and crew accommodations were correspondingly large. Because *Liberator* was designed to stay submerged nearly all the time, a lot of effort went into designing comfortable living spaces. Most American nuclear submarines were comfortable in comparison to their conventionally powered ancestors, because the nuclear power plant took up so much less space than a diesel propulsion system with its bulky fuel tanks and battery space. *Liberator* was almost luxurious, designed to be a home away from home, a seaborne colony as well as a warship. Space was also important because, with a few exceptions, her crew was older than the norm, better paid and better trained. Such men and women would not likely be attracted by Spartan accommodations. Everyone had his own cabin and the officers their own heads and showers. There was no old-Navy hot-bunking aboard *Liberator*, and since the ship was so highly computerized, everyone had his own monitor (for use in recreational viewing as well as in monitoring ship's systems).

In all, *Liberator* was the first submarine constructed to be a home and research laboratory as well as a ship. She was almost entirely self-sufficient and could prowl the world at will, exploring as well as defending herself and the nation. Her existence presumed a new era of submarine life, one where military significance timeshared with global research and undersea living.

Thomas P. Donovan was a wise choice as her captain. The thirty-seven-year-old son of a highly decorated New York City police detective, he mixed nautical savvy with a mild temperament that instilled confidence in the crew. Donovan cut his teeth on Los Angeles–class submarines, where he rose to the rank of captain and enjoyed his first command. He was given the helm of *Liberator* because of his combination of experience, temperament, and adaptability. He had little problem adjusting to new conditions, and that was a quality judged of vast importance to the commander of a radically new design of submarine.

As he sat in the captain's chair behind the helm, Donovan watched the Cyclops display: white-blue glimmers of light from the surface above, blue-black open water to port, starboard and ahead, and black below the ship, with the flat bottom of the sea being displayed as a hint of lime green that showed few features. Donovan couldn't get over the view. It reminded him of video games he'd played on the Upper West Side of Manhattan as a kid, the games where you drove a spaceship through a tunnel of light and sound. Only this time the game was real, and the white-blue light above him was filtered through 200 feet of water that was crammed with plankton and sharks.

John Percy, the executive officer, pointed out a

twenty-foot blip that whizzed by the hull, tiny numbers alongside it showing its dimensions.

"A great white shark, if I'm not mistaken," he said. "There are lots of them in these waters."

Alex added, "There are lots more than there should be. Readings of large shark and whale species are many times what they should be."

"It's a repeat of San Francisco," Donovan said, referring to their visit to the remains of that city in the days immediately after World War Three, where among other things they found a proliferation of large, nasty animals; wolves, in that case.

The Cyclops display showed numerous large sea creatures to port and starboard and ahead, most in the prime life zone down to twenty fathoms but some at considerable depths. Most swam alone, but in the waters near the edge of the abyssal trench a cluster of sharks surrounded a much larger carcass.

Helmsman Hooper said, "Maintaining forty knots, distance to the atoll is seven thousand yards."

"Is anything out there?" Donovan asked.

"Negative, Captain," said Communications Officer Jennings. "Nothing on sonar, nothing on laser. I now have been searching for three hours, results all negative."

"What are we looking for?" Alex asked.

"*Nemesis*."

"Not her again! What makes you think she's still in the South Pacific?"

"We are always looking for her," Donovan said. "We haven't heard from her in a month. That's longer than she's ever left us alone. I have a feeling it's wise to always be ready for her, especially now she's been gone so long."

"We don't even know who she is."

"We know what she sounds like," Donovan said. "Mr. Jennings, repeat scan: any noise of any kind that resembles our own."

"Aye, Captain. Listening for *Nemesis*'s screw signature, which is to say, *Liberator*'s screw signature."

Percy said, "This is really crazy, listening for our own noises."

"I agree," Donovan said. "It's quite impossible for another sub to duplicate our screw signature, not to mention our turbine sounds. But this one does. Mr. Hooper, do you see that island?"

"It's in sight, Captain. Five thousand yards to the coral reef."

"Captain's intuition—put up an icon for *Nemesis* and position it behind the island."

"What makes you think she's there?" Percy asked, as a yellow-green miniature of a submarine abruptly appeared on the Cyclops display along with the notation "potential enemy."

Donovan folded his arms and said, "Because that's where I would be lurking, were I hiding from us. Slow to one-half. Mr. Percy, load tubes one and two, proximity fuse, magnetic and laser targeting."

"We'll get her this time, Captain," Executive Officer Percy swore.

The book on the young man, barely thirty, was that he was hotheaded, and so he had been passed over for command several times. It was said he longed too much for the glory days of armed combat at sea, when tours of duty were all guns-blazing shootouts with steel. Such days had mostly been forgotten, and even World War Three had been fought and finished without anyone raising a pen to write about it. If it was glorious, no one lived to recall it.

But Percy dreamed of the glory of war and excelled at war games, even though he lacked the depth of temperament needed to be a submarine commander, or so believed the admirals who thought that a year or two under Donovan would mellow Percy for command. Donovan found him an able officer with a lot of eagerness for the job. Sometimes it was hard to get him off the bridge, and he certainly didn't subscribe to the one-shift-on, two-shifts-off design for *Liberator* officers.

The real zealot among the crew was Dave Hooper, the nineteen-year-old helmsman. While all officers felt they had a personal stake in the ship, Hooper claimed actual ownership and knew more about her systems than anyone, with the possible exception of Carl "Flazy" Smith, the chief engineer. Hooper and Smith, whose nickname meant "fat and lazy," spent most of their time arguing who knew more about *Liberator*. Smith probably knew more, having participated in crucial design decisions, but Hooper spoke louder and was seated closer to the captain, who found the "who's most loyal" contest amusing.

Donovan peered at the Cyclops display. "Anything on sensors, Mr. Jennings?" he asked.

"Just normal background noise, Captain. Fish and marine mammals. Some echoes off the bottom sediment from our own prop."

"When are we going to have a way of filtering that out?"

"As soon as you set me up in a decent lab, *Captain*," Alex said. "One on *land*."

She was a brilliant software engineer and Ph.D. who knew more about computers than anyone aboard. With her brother, now the ship's surgeon, she came aboard as one of the San Francisco survivors and was charged mainly with helping them set up housekeeping in a suitable South Pacific island, as soon as they found one.

But the search was on hold. Donovan's intuition told him that *Nemesis* was in that neck of the woods, and would almost certainly be spoiling for a fight. From the immediate postwar days, *Nemesis* haunted Donovan's dreams. No one knew who she was. She looked and sounded like *Liberator*, and at first had employed bioacoustic damping to mask engine and prop sounds. She was faster than the American sub, though, and Donovan's brother Charlie, the first to get a glimpse of her, thought she was responsible for starting World War Three. A debate raged whether she was Russian or a warship of newly reunited Germany. The greatest debate was over her intentions. In several encounters with *Liberator* she had only harassed the American ship, then run away. What did she want?

Donovan couldn't answer that question, but knew that he didn't want any interruptions now that they were so close to finding a secure island harbor to call home. That had been their goal ever since they realized their responsibility as the only existing powerful force in the world—to do what they could to help survivors. For that they would need a secure base, and various computer models showed that the South Pacific was the best place to look for one. Alex Fisher thought that the Society Islands, in particular, were the place to look, and the *Liberator* was on course for them. The crew had searched unsuccessfully for safe harbor along the way. The Marshalls had been volcanically unstable; the Gilbert Islands had no deep water bay. At the moment, circling back through the Marshalls, the Society Islands ahead were their best and last hope, but Donovan could not keep them in his mind. The hairs on the back of his arms were tingling, a sure sign that something indefinable was wrong.

Sensing this, Dave Jennings, who was both communications officer and Cyclops operator, said: "There's nothing out there, Skipper. Nothing but a whole lot of hungry sharks and one carcass."

"No *Nemesis*?"

"Not unless she's maintaining utter silence and hiding behind that island."

"It's not impossible," Percy said.

"Distance to the island?" Donovan asked.

"Four thousand yards to the first line of coral," Hooper replied.

"Reduce speed to one-quarter and take us around the northern side of the island."

"Aye, Captain."

"There's something wrong. I can feel it."

"What's wrong?" Alex asked.

"We're so *alone*."

"You had better get used to it."

"I *am*. What I'm not used to is the feeling that someone is hiding in that silence, waiting to kill me. If only *Nemesis* had a face."

Percy agreed. "It's tough enough to be shot at. It's worse when you don't know who's pulling the trigger."

"Or why," Donovan said, leaning forward. "Mr. Jennings, are you sure you're getting nothing on sensors?"

"Nothing unusual, Captain. Normal sea noises and echoes."

" 'Normal' according to whom?"

Alex perked up, and said, "Right! The memory banks for echo analysis are based on submarine tracks laid down in the North Atlantic and North Pacific over flat terrain or subsea ridges. There is no memory on runs over submarine trenches."

"What does *that* mean?" Hooper asked.

"It means that our software designers never figured we'd be fighting in trench terrain," Donovan said.

"What trench?"

"That one," the captain replied, pointing at the representation of the Marshall Trench to starboard, where the sea abruptly dropped off to a depth of three miles.

"And, because they never thought we'd be fighting in this part of the sea, they never gave us memory of what echoes off trench walls sound like," Alex said.

Donovan pointed at Jennings, and said, "Make a laser profile of the trench from amidships to four miles ahead. Bounce the beams off the far wall. Make some noise and read the echoes."

"Aye, Captain," Jennings said, and a few seconds later, laser pulses from the hull-mounted projector swept through the ocean depths and echoed off the near rim and far wall of the Marshall Trench. A flurry of data was displayed at the communications officer's station, then interpreted by the software.

"Echoes off the far wall, Captain. It's our screw signature, but displaced by ten point two-seven-seven miles, which is the distance between us and the far trench wall."

"Is it an exact match?"

"Aye, Captain . . . couldn't be more exact."

"Is there anything near the rim on this side?" Donovan asked.

"Nope. I can give you a distance figure and a close-up picture if you like. Wait . . . getting something."

All eyes turned toward the communications officer

and Alex Fisher, who had joined him at his station and was interpreting data.

"What is it?"

"A partial harmonic. Maybe an echo off our echo. It's localized just beyond the trench rim at about two hundred thirty-seven degrees . . . moving as we move."

Donovan felt the chill at the back of his neck. "Alert stations!" he called. "Mr. Percy, stand ready on your torpedoes! Mr. Hooper, ahead full, come right to two-four-five! Dive to one thousand feet the second we're over the trench!"

"*Nemesis*, Captain?" Percy asked.

"I'll bet a month's pay on it."

Liberator leaped forward, her T7W steam turbines pouring energy against the sea and pushing the titanium-composite hull ahead at speeds only dreamed of a generation earlier.

"Torpedoes are armed, magnetic and laser targeting, proximity fuses set for one hundred yards."

"Reset laser to weapons status."

"Weapons status remains a question mark on the lasers, Captain," Percy said.

"I haven't had the time to fix the targeting so they can be used against torpedoes," Alex said. "The aiming mechanism won't hold on something that small for long enough to disrupt circuits."

"Yet another problem for you to solve once you get your lab," Donovan said, meaning that it was also yet another promise for her to deliver on.

"Then what target shall we use for the lasers?" Percy asked.

"Amidships on *Nemesis*, same as the time we fought her outside San Francisco Bay. The lasers were good enough to knock out that bioacoustic damping that was letting her run silently with only a fourteen-twenty hertz drone. This ability she has to duplicate our sounds may be another trick."

"If they can trick us on bioacoustics, they can trick us on sound replication," Alex agreed.

"Whoever they are, they seem to be good on tricks,"

Donovan said. "I have one of my own—we'll dip into the trench behind her and fire from dead astern. Nail her before she can get away."

"Too late," Jennings said. "That echo off the echo I got? It's increased in RPM, matching our own increase in speed. But it's not an exact match. That's *Nemesis* all right, but she heard us speed up and is doing the same."

"We're getting her on sonar now," Alex added.

"Putting her on the screen."

All bridge hands watched as the icon that had represented *Nemesis* disappeared from behind the coral atoll and was positioned in the trench, running north up the near side of the trench, getting away.

"Dammit," Donovan swore. "Mr. Hooper, put the pedal to the metal. Distance to target?"

"Twenty thousand yards and increasing," Hooper replied. "*Nemesis* is making fifty knots and pulling away."

"She's still faster than us," Jennings said.

"We'll see about that," Hooper replied, pushing the annunciator forward until it nearly broke off. Donovan swore he could hear Chief Smith in the engine room, cursing at the turbines.

"She's almost out of torpedo range," Percy said.

"She accelerates faster than us," Donovan admitted.

"We're at fifty knots," Hooper announced.

"She's at fifty-five," Jennings replied.

"A torpedo shot is no longer possible, Captain. We could use a missile."

The Mark 97N missiles came with a field-grade nuclear warhead that was first tested in the Central American War of the 1990s. It could take out a square mile on dry land and make a somewhat larger chunk of water highly inhospitable. But it wasn't proven against submerged targets. Its use as a naval weapon was always figured to be against carrier groups or solitary large surface vessels. Donovan had already used up one of the twenty-four that *Liberator* sailed with.

He shook his head. "The future will be long and we

have no replacements," he said. "Missiles have to be conserved."

"*Nemesis* is making sixty knots and has topped out," Hooper said, adding, quickly, "Apparently."

"And our speed?"

"Fifty-eight and increasing. We can catch her, Captain."

"After a chase of a thousand miles, maybe. Break it off, Mr. Hooper."

"But, *Captain!*"

"I understand, but do what I say anyway. Mr. Jennings, keep a sharp sensor watch on the target. Let's make sure she stays well away from us. This time when we go to resume the search for our base I don't want her anywhere around."

In the months since the end of the world, *Liberator* had one main goal: to do what she could to help survivors of World War Three. To that end, Donovan had decided to seek a secure base far from the continents, which according to the best evidence were all infested with white-shirts—zombielike ghouls racked by radiation psychosis and given to prowling the ruins of civilization killing all in their path.

The white-shirts were first encountered in the Aleutians just two weeks after the war and quickly swept down the Pacific Coast of North America, reaching Seattle and California in record time. *Liberator* fought them all the way down the coast, using her first tactical nuclear missile to destroy a large and bloodthirsty group of them in San Francisco.

There was no hard evidence of white-shirts elsewhere in the world, but a computer analysis by Alex suggested that white-shirts were almost certainly a widespread consequence of World War Three. Where there was enough radiation, radiation psychosis was the result. Enough cases of that especially nasty disease resulted in bands of white-shirts, who were like homicidal lemmings in their mindless attacks on all living things.

Donovan believed the computer projection of white-shirts everywhere on the continents, and that was yet another reason for his decision to base *Liberator* on an island, away from major land masses. It would be hard enough coping with life in the aftermath of Armageddon in places like China, Australia, South America, Europe and Africa. It would be nearly impossible to stay long in those places if white-shirts had to be battled as well.

Donovan also knew that his visits to formerly populated areas had to be selective as well as brief. In the months since the war, they had encountered only two other functioning ships—*Nemesis* and the Russian submarine *Charkov*, which they had fought successfully. Computer analysis suggested that only a few ships survived: *Liberator* by virtue of being under the north polar ice pack at the time of the war, and *Charkov* by a fluke. No one knew how *Nemesis* survived, but since there was some evidence that she had a hand in starting the conflagration, it was assumed that she had a way of surviving it.

Donovan felt pretty sure that *Liberator* and *Nemesis* were alone in the sea, and that no other power of any kind threatened. No surface ships had survived, and only one old plane that they knew of. To the best of all knowledge, *Liberator* and her mysterious shadow were the sole surviving military powers in the world.

There was so much for *Liberator* to do; the process of picking up the pieces would last years and take them all over the globe. Already, one group of survivors was en route from San Francisco to the South Pacific on board a 120-year-old schooner, *Priscilla*. The plan was to link up with the schooner and have the crew of *Liberator* join with the survivors in creating a new society on an island home.

That home would also serve as a base for *Liberator*'s worldwide rescue operations. As foreseen by Donovan, *Liberator* would respond to distress calls and go wherever she was needed, taking advantage of a central location—convenient for fast steaming to any part of the Pacific rim, or into the Atlantic through Panama, an area of interest itself. One of Donovan's priorities was to find out the status of the Panama Canal and go through it to the Atlantic, for a voyage of discovery up the East Coast.

Liberator had escorted *Priscilla* to the South Pacific as well as scouting islands herself since leaving San Francisco, and had been distracted only by the battle with the Russian submarine and encounters with *Nemesis*. Now she was free to voyage to the last uninspected group of islands, the Society Islands, to consummate the search for a new home.

Jennings spent an hour assuring himself that *Nemesis* was gone for a while. Her pattern was to make an appearance, be chased off, then disappear for a few days or weeks, and this time so far seemed no different. Still, *Liberator* occupied herself in precautionary silent running maneuvers past the coast of Eniwetok, where the early thermonuclear weapons tests were made in the 1950s. At the same time, Alex used the laser's scientific probe capacity to take surface temperature and other measurements, including radiation.

Donovan watched her fondly for a while before turning to Jennings. "Mr. Jennings, have we lost *Nemesis*?"

"There is no trace of her, Captain. The sea is clear once again."

"Very well. Mr. Hooper, set course for Papeete in the Society Islands. I have always wanted to go to Tahiti."

Alex said, "The computer suggests that the population of the Polynesian Islands was affected like that of the Marshalls—reduced but not wiped out. There may be room for us."

"There may be room for all of us. Status of *Priscilla*?"

"Our last radio report from her puts her south of Fatu Hiva in the Marquesas," Jennings said. "She's sailing west-southwest and making eight knots under sail, having picked up a good tail wind three days ago."

"Let's hope it holds. Time to rendezvous at Papeete?"

"Three days at her present speed. She should be crossing through the Tuamoto group south of King George Island sometime in the next ten hours. Our next radio contact with her is scheduled for thirteen hundred hours tomorrow."

"We'll get to Papeete ahead of her and check it out,"

Donovan said. "Mr. Hooper, ahead full on the course we laid out this morning."

"Aye, Captain. Ahead full."

The bridge annunciator—an anachronism that everyone in the crew agreed was a pleasant reminder of the classic days of steamships—rang full ahead as the ship leapt forward.

Donovan got up from his position and stretched. "Mr. Percy, you have the con. I'm going to take a shower."

Donovan recalled taking his first shower as a boy on the *West Wind*, the elegant old wooden yacht that his father and mother lived aboard during warm weather. That was berthed at the 79th Street Boat Basin, on New York's Upper West Side, where the elder Donovan was one of the city's most decorated police detectives. Memories of that boat helped forge Thomas Donovan's resolve to go to sea, and as he showered in his cabin aboard *Liberator* he still was unable to get those old thoughts out of his head.

They were all dead, of course, his parents as well as everything else he knew and loved. All that remained of his family was his kid brother, Charlie, who at that moment slept in his own cabin down the hall. Charlie was the first person rescued by *Liberator* after emerging from the north polar ice pack, where she had been testing her ability to evade detection and which had shielded her from the war. Charlie had flown on the LAMPS helicopter that was chasing *Nemesis* when she fired the missile generally blamed with having touched off World War Three. The chopper was downed in the Bering Strait and Charlie was plucked from a life raft, the first person encountered by the *Liberator* crew.

The soap ran down Donovan's face and stung his eyes. Soap, he thought; another irreplaceable commodity. Or, rather, one that would have to be manufactured once they found a base. There were so many adjustments to be made. They would need a supply of staples like soap, paper, a source of clean water, and food. Access to plants that had medicinal value. *Liberator*'s nuclear reactor made plenty of energy. That was a resource good for the indefinite future. But soap . . . yet another thing to add to the list of stuff they would soon run out of.

"Is this the last Coke?" Alex asked. He heard the door of the minifridge shut.

"Take it," Donovan called out.

"Take your last Coke?"

"Everyone else ran out a week ago. I was saving it for a special occasion."

She asked, "What's special about this? Every day is like every other."

"We're en route to the Society Islands again and will finally get there. We can play Adam and Eve like we planned. Why aren't you on the bridge?"

"Because I'm tired, same as you. I'm taking the Coke."

She opened it, the hiss reminding Donovan of the sparkle of cold sodas and beers popped open on the Fourth of July. Something else that would never happen again. Fourth of July celebrations with soda and beer.

He came out of the shower toweling off, walked to where she sat on the bunk, and took a sip from her bottle.

"Not bad-looking for an old guy," she said, patting his wet tummy.

"I'm only thirty-seven," he complained. "The youngest captain in the service."

"The *only* captain in the service."

"A minor point. Once we get on land we can do some running. You do run, don't you?"

"Only from bill collectors, and they're all dead. Donovan, once we find a home you'll be too busy working to have to go looking for exercise."

"Working?" he said, mouthing the word as if it contained broken glass.

"Yeah, working. Picking up coconuts. Building shelters. Cutting logs. Working."

He tossed the towel back into the head and pulled

on a pair of casual slacks. "I'm the boss," he said. "I supervise."

"We'll see. Anyway, I've refined the search for habitable islands to the point where the list is now workable. There are three candidates within two days' sailing—that's two days on *Priscilla*—from Papeete. All of them are prime: the right size, the right climate, and not overpopulated."

"Good harbors?" he asked, pulling on a shirt.

"One harbor is excellent. Maybe a bit shallow, about twenty feet mean depth."

"That's a little shallow. Do we have charts?"

"Not as such. They're not common ports of call. We have satellite photos from which I have deduced features like depth of water and types of vegetation. Habitations. Another has no natural harbor, but does have a narrow channel between the two main islands. That reads as being forty feet deep, but there may be a problem with currents. They look persistent and strong."

"Submarines do not dock well in strange currents," Donovan said. "And we need a place from which we can make fast getaways."

"The third island is the caldera of an extinct volcano adjacent to a volcano that shows recent activity."

"Great. An island that may explode."

"It could, especially since the war. We've already seen increased volcanism in the South Pacific, which has always been a seismically active area anyway."

"Is there an up side to this island?"

"Yeah. The caldera is a mile wide and essentially bottomless. All you have to do is blast a hole in one wall and you have a harbor that men and nations would die for. You can do that, can't you?"

"Probably. What's the rock like, volcanic?"

"That and coral, I would imagine. It's damned fertile. You should see the abundance of vegetation."

"We'll check it out, but it sounds good."

"And only two days' sail from Tahiti."

"Why has no one discovered it before?"

"They have. There's a small settlement, probably

holding four or five hundred people. But this island is not on the way to anyplace. As far as island residents go, it's on the edge of the known universe—halfway to Pitcairn, which is where the *Bounty* mutineers settled down."

"Smaller islands were developed."

"This one has no landing strip or the capability for one. It's too far away for casual commerce and the waters are full of sharks. As far as Pacific islanders are concerned, this place is of minor importance. For a submarine crew that just wants to be left alone to live in peace, it's ideal."

"Does it have a name?" Donovan asked.

"Espiritu," she replied, handing him the empty Coke bottle to throw out for her.

Donovan watched bemusedly as his brother strained against the Nautilus machine, dragging the bar down and pressing it against his chest, beads of sweat breaking out all over.

"Is there some reason that this machine is any better than chinning yourself on a steam pipe?" he asked.

"Yeah, I don't have to worry about banging my head on these low ceilings," Charlie replied. "Besides, if I broke a pipe in this ship I'd probably sink her."

"Don't flatter yourself, son."

"Lateral pull-downs are better on the machine. You ought to try it."

"Does everyone think I'm out of shape? I plan to run on the beach . . . once we find ourselves a beach."

"You're middle-aged, slugger. It's time for you to take a wife and settle down. Go out into the fields and gather roots and tubers for dinner."

"And pick up coconuts. She got to you, didn't she?"

"Who? Our science officer?"

"Yeah, her. She's been lobbying for me to settle down and build huts on this island we haven't even seen yet. Espiritu, it's called."

"She did mention the island," Charlie admitted, switching from lateral pull-downs to bench presses. "It's supposed to be nice."

"Paradise with sharks and an active volcano. Probably there's a forty-foot monkey with a bad temperament living there, too."

"I love it. Lighten up, big brother. She wants her man to settle down and act normal. Every woman wants that."

"I'm a submarine captain and we're living in the wake of World War Three," Donovan said. "Life on the run *is* normal."

Charlie finished his workout and wiped his face on a towel. "Are you planning any surface running on the way to Tahiti? I want to work on my tan."

Donovan blanched, and was about to start a ruckus when Executive Officer Percy's voice came over the speakers:

"Captain to the bridge! Surface contact, bearing zero-six-nine!"

"Do you tan fast?" he asked, starting aft.

"Faster than you'd ever believe," Charlie said, chasing after him.

Hooper was at the helm with Percy looking over his shoulder at the Cyclops display, when Donovan and Charlie ran onto the bridge.

"What do you have?" Donovan asked, taking the captain's chair.

"Single contact, Captain. A ship, distance fourteen miles and closing."

"Come to course zero-six-nine. Periscope depth."

"Zero-six-nine, coming to periscope depth."

"Mr. Jennings, is she making any noise?"

"Not a sound, Captain. And I'm getting no sonar registry plate—she's not one of ours."

"Put her on the screen," Donovan ordered. He bent forward to look at the Cyclops screen. A blip appeared on the horizon, just a blur at first, then as *Liberator* drew nearer and came closer to the surface, it was clarified into a ship icon floating on the surface, apparently dead in the water.

"More readings, Captain. There's no engines, no sonar or depth sounding, and the only heat generation is the temperature differential with the surface water. She's as dead as they come."

"She's not playing dead?"

"I get no more thermal readings than would be generated by a floating log."

Charlie agreed, "She's dead."

"Is this your legendary intuition?" Donovan asked.

"Yeah. What of it?"

"What is our present location?"

"In the deep water between Nanumea Island in the Ellice group and Winslow Reef in the Phoenix Islands," Percy reported. "We just crossed the international date line—if that makes a difference."

"It doesn't," Donovan said, adding, "This bit of sea is between left field and nowhere. How long is that hulk?"

"Five hundred fifty feet, more or less," Jennings reported.

"It could be a destroyer. But *whose* destroyer? The Polynesian navy ain't noted for heavy artillery."

Jennings said, "Target is now seven miles and closing."

"We're at periscope depth," Percy said.

"Slow to one-quarter. Any more readings?"

"She's still quiet. Not even funeral dirges are playing."

"Raise periscope and antenna mast."

He waited while his order was carried out and Jennings used the radar receiver to check for signals coming from above the surface. The communications officer shook his head. "No signals, Captain."

Donovan swept the horizon with the periscope, then focused on the ship, making his own observations as well as pressing the button that videotaped what he saw.

The ship was a shade over 550 feet and with narrow beam, a destroyer or destroyer escort, but one that had been savaged by the war in the same way as the other ships that *Liberator* had encountered. "A small warship, maybe a destroyer," Donovan reported. "It could be Japanese, and in any event is burned to the waterline. This is the same thing we saw in the North

Pacific. So much for any notion that Polynesia escaped the war."

The ship looked like putty that had been melted down to the waterline, with only a few sharp angles and semistanding masts to remind one that it used to be a ship.

"Take readings, Mr. Jennings. Same as before: figure out from wind and drift how far that boat has come since she was dead in the water. Correlate this data with what we observed before. We'll write a history of the war yet."

"Aye, Captain. But we could do more if we had a full science crew aboard."

"Do you want to surface and look at her?" Percy asked.

"I certainly do. Down scope and antennas. Mr. Hooper, bring her up."

The bridge crew watched as the automated control systems brought *Liberator* flawlessly to the surface. When the upper bridge broke the surface and a crewman opened the hatch, Donovan was the first topsides. Charlie broke out of the hatch and onto the foredeck, brandishing the Navy version of the Luigi Franchi 9-mm automatic, followed by Alex and Percy.

The compact submachine gun had a 32-round box magazine, an 8-inch barrel, and a 250-round cyclic rate of fire when on automatic. The Franchi was constructed from rectangular welded tubing for easy handling by machine shops that did not have advanced manufacturing capabilities, and for years was favored by guerilla groups in Latin America, Africa, and Southeast Asia. It was issued to sub crews because it was repairable in their machine shops. Whimsically appointed First Gunnery Officer by his brother, Charlie was a fantastic shot and good as leader of the ship's small arms party.

The teal-colored hull of *Liberator* moved swiftly and in near silence across the placid surface of the South Pacific. Her lines were gently rounded, like the back of a porpoise, and even the four torpedo tubes and the planes blended into the ship's overall gracefulness, which was made even more pronounced by the silence of her motion. *Liberator* spoke of power and control, and the feel of her running on the surface thrilled all aboard.

A bridge lookout cried "Ship dead ahead, four miles."

All eyes shifted in that direction. Through the binoculars Donovan made out the scarred lines and tattered insignia of a Royal Australian Navy guided missile destroyer, the *Endara*.

"She's a thousand miles from home," Donovan said. "And none of these islands are Australian protectorates. What gives?"

The sea was littered with flotsam. A small slick of debris bobbed quietly in the still water, surrounding the drifting hulk with a halo of ship's junk. Outside this circle the Pacific was calm and clean. Inside was a different matter. It was a vision of sailor hell, with death and corruption and not even the dignity of a sunken grave.

"My God," Donovan said as *Liberator* swept quietly by.

"It's the same thing we saw off Vancouver." Percy's anger sounded in the snarl of his voice.

"There can't be any survivors."

Alex shook her head. "The heat outside the hull of this ship was high enough to vaporize the crew."

Dr. Fisher arrived on deck to witness the latest wreckage. "The wreck is hot," he said. "There's too much radiation for us to go in, except in protective suits."

"What about this area of sea?" Donovan asked.

"There's a lot of radiation within the flotsam diameter. We shouldn't stick around too long."

Liberator passed close enough to the bow of *Endara* to see details of the heat scarring. The underside of the prow was scorched in a pattern that resembled ivy on a brick wall.

Charlie was on the foredeck, where the topside curve reached its height before plummeting to the bow, cradling his Franchi and staring at the ruined destroyer.

Donovan said, "Mr. Percy, have Mr. Jennings speed up that drift analysis. Let's see how long and far the ship drifted from her original position."

"Aye, Captain."

"And Mr. Percy, put us back on course for Papeete."

"On the surface?"

"Yes. We all need some air. Topside leave for off-duty personnel, in parties of six."

Percy saluted and went below.

Liberator came around approximately South-Southwest and as she picked up speed, water began to crash over the bow. By the time the ship was again in the open sea, only the topside bridge and a stretch of deck fore and aft of it stayed dry.

Donovan stayed topsides with the lookouts to let the salt spray off the Pacific soak his hair, clothes and skin. After a while, Charlie joined him, then Alex. With his woman under his arm and his brother by his side, he stayed above in the spray as *Liberator* slipped into a glorious Pacific sunset.

5

The horizon was thin as a pencil line and curved slightly, a powder blue sky disappearing in all directions into a blue sea. There were no clouds. No islands could be seen. No birds or insects were in the sky. By the look of things, *Liberator* was near landfall on nothing. They were truly at the edge of the world and at risk of falling off.

Finally, though, the horizon ahead of the ship thickened, the pencil line drawing darker and greener and finally bulging up to show the 7,352-foot peak of Mount Orohena. Tahiti grew up from the horizon and broadened, and before long the horizon stretched to show the Tairapu Peninsula to the southeast and Moorea Island to the northwest.

Donovan resisted the temptation to yell "Land ho," but would have been quick to admit that it was the first thing that came to his mind.

All ship's sensors showed no sign of human activity. Radar, sonar, and UHF radio revealed nothing. As was the case with *Liberator*'s approaches to the northwest coast of the United States, silence was the rule of the day.

"Lookouts keep an eye out for boats, planes . . . anything," Donovan said as watch officers flooded onto the topside bridge. The ship drew closer to the tropical island and swung around the northern shore toward Papeete, but the only activity came from seabirds and flying fish.

High-powered optics showed surf breaking over a coral line that was exposed by an outgoing tide and, finally, unbroken white sand that circled the island like a band of pearls. Peter Fisher, Alex's brother, came topsides and made atmospheric tests, principally background radiation. He too found nothing out of the ordinary.

It was a summer morning and nothing was happening on the pearl of the South Pacific. As *Liberator* cruised slowly toward the capital, the lookouts continued to watch for signs of man but nothing was found. Tahiti had retained its ageless pristine beauty, despite a coastline well-developed by man, and gave every impression of being as primitive as it was the day the *Bounty* dropped her hook offshore.

"This is another Dutch Harbor," Donovan said.

"The city in the Aleutians?" Alex asked, understanding the reference.

"Yeah. It was our first port of call after sailing out from under the polar ice pack. The first big town we encountered. There was no sign of civilization there, either. It was deserted."

"Save for the white-shirts," Charlie added.

"You can't think that they're in Tahiti, too!" Alex said, alarmed.

"I hope not. The odds are good that they can't swim."

"And would be eaten by sharks if they tried," Charlie added, noting several ominous gray figures that swam near the starboard beam.

"If the white-shirts aren't here, what are the people hiding from?"

"Us, maybe," Donovan said.

"Maybe they're dead."

"If that were true there would be radiation," Dr. Fisher said.

"Not to mention bodies on the beach."

"They're not dead," Charlie said. "I can feel it. Unfortunately, I can't say what happened to them."

"What's the computer projection for war effects in this part of the world?"

"Hazy," Alex reported. "The best model I have calls for sporadic effects in the South Pacific, rather like what happens when tornadoes touch down. One block is destroyed and the one right next to it is untouched. There's no evidence of radiation here, but no sign of people, either. I just don't know what happened. Will we set foot on land?"

"I didn't sail all the way to Tahiti just to wave at it and go away," Donovan said. "We'll put ashore in Papeete and scout around. Maybe something there will tell us what happened to everyone."

"In Dutch Harbor the white-shirts killed the survivors," Charlie warned.

"There can't be any white-shirts here," Donovan said firmly. "But the lack of people is damned peculiar."

As *Liberator* circled the island, keeping the nearly circular shoreline to port, lookouts as well as electronic sensors watched for signs of human life. There were many signs of prior habitation—roads, docks, empty boats, apartment houses, private homes, seaplane docks, even an occasional mansion—but not one soul. Cars sat abandoned on the coastal highway. Even the many motor scooters and minibikes sat where their owners abandoned them, often in the middle of the street. Once they saw a twin-hulled pirogue teetering half on the beach and half on the tide, in danger of floating out to sea, its owner nowhere to be found.

Papeete appeared suddenly, thrust out of the jungle and looking like an eighteenth-century village gone slightly mad with twenty-first century buildings, docks, and antennae. It still had an old, shabby look, and the many tin-roofed houses seemed as if they were sagging under the weight of the tropical sun. The harbor, built for the trade in dried coconut meat and upgraded to hold freighters from Japan and Los Angeles as well as yachts from a hundred wealthy nations, had an aura of disrespect. It was as if a press-gang could at any time pop out from behind an office building and shanghai an unsuspecting sailor into years of servitude.

"I wonder if Quinn's is still there," Jennings asked, a faraway look in his eye.

"What's that? A bar?"

He nodded. "A dive, notorious from Beveridge Reef to Disappointment Island."

"We must check it out," Donovan said, half-interested.

"I always wanted to settle down and tend bar at Quinn's."

"This may be your chance. Mr. Percy, we'll anchor half a mile from the dock at the end of Boulevard Pomare and go in by small boat. I'll need a small arms party. The chief gunnery officer will lead it."

"Yes, sir," Charlie said, going below for his Franchi and some ammunition.

"I'll be going ashore and taking Chief Smith, Mr. Jennings, and both Doctors Fisher—Alex to see if Papeete fits the computer model for war effects, and her brother to check the radiation and look for more clues regarding radiation psychosis. Clearly something weird has happened here."

"Clearly," Percy agreed.

Donovan scanned the harbor, and his gaze settled on the fleet of elegant, million-dollar transoceanic sailing yachts that were moored at the Royal Tahitian Yacht Club. Some of them were over 100 feet long and all were perfectly capable of making fast passages under sail across thousands of miles of sea.

"While I'm onshore, why don't you look into the feasibility of liberating some of this wonderful hardware. I'm madly in love with *Priscilla*, but she can only make eight knots and can only carry a few people comfortably. Considering our future needs for wind-borne transportation..."

"Consider a few good boats liberated, Captain."

"We can get a nice little fleet together by the time *Priscilla* arrives tomorrow," Donovan said.

"And use it to check out all three prospective island bases simultaneously," Percy said.

* * *

The two semirigid inflatables moved slowly away from the hull of *Liberator* and across the mirror-smooth water of the harbor. To the port side was the deep water channel leading up to the main commercial dock, where half a dozen freighters and numerous tugs and tenders were tied up. Off the starboard beam was the Royal Tahitian Yacht Club, a late-nineteenth-century wooden mansion with a single long pier to which twenty yachts were tied, resembling grapes on the vine. Ahead was the stubby tourist pier at the end of tree-lined Boulevard Pomare, a fancy street that inevitably showed up in postcards and tourist snapshots.

Squatting in the bow of his boat, Donovan cradled a Franchi and was comforted by the steel of a Colt automatic in its holster. Twenty yards away, Charlie stood boldly in the boat he commanded, seeming to dare any sniper to take a shot at him. He was, after all, the marksman in the family. A two-time Navy pistol champion, his expertise was guessing where and when targets would pop up and then plugging them. With his legendary intuition, Donovan's kid brother was the best at riding shotgun into the unknown.

Donovan's boat sidled up to the pier at the point where a floating dock was connected to a ladder up to the quay. "This reminds me of Fisherman's Wharf," Donovan said, looking at Alex to confirm that it stirred the same memory in her.

The dock was built at the end of the twentieth century as a spot for tourists to gather for cocktails and lunch and also to take photos of the pirogues and other native canoes that were paddled by. A handful of the twin-hulled dugouts floated farther down the pier.

Donovan led the way onto the quay, looked around, and said, "Alone again. Dammit, where the hell is everyone in this world?"

"Missing in action," Charlie said.

"If this is another Dutch Harbor we can expect a white-shirt attack from the dockside buildings. Watch the rooftops and alleys."

"There's no one here," Charlie said emphatically.

"Just to be safe."

"Trust me. We're alone, like you said. Damned if I know what happened to the population, but they ain't around."

Peter Fisher's hand-held EnviroTester sniffed the hot summer air, and he reported, "No evidence of significant background radiation. I need to check the water supply and some local fruits and vegetables, though."

"What do you expect to find?"

"Don't know. But the population didn't just split for no reason. There may be some weird radiation effect we've never seen before."

"You don't think that radiation psychosis is in the South Pacific, too."

"I don't expect it with the same degree of severity. On the continental land masses, the principal symptom is homicidal psychosis, which we have come to call whiteshirt behavior. On the islands, radiation psychosis may take another form. We simply won't know until we do more tests—and meet some of the residents."

"Where are they?" Donovan mused, looking nervously at the rooftops and alleys of the harbor area.

Moving in single file, with Charlie in the lead, they left the pier and stepped onto the two-laned, paved harbor road. Shops stood on one side and port facilities on the other side of the road, which zigged and zagged its way around the harbor.

Donovan peered into a 2003 Toyota that stood at an intersection. It was dead in the middle of the road, its doors locked and the windows up. Behind it was a 1999 Honda in a similar state, and halfway out of a cross street was a battered Chevy truck that also had been locked and left.

The stores were also locked. All over Papeete, the citizenry had locked the doors and left. Even the many motorbikes and scooters had their ignitions locked. Charlie wandered up to a tiny shop that sold *firi-firi*, a kind of doughnut, the Tahitian equivalent of fast food. All the windows in the little shop were closed, probably for the first time in years. Any Tahitian store with large ovens was certainly never closed up entirely, because of the constant heat. But these were, all of them.

"This is different from the Aleutians," Donovan said. "There, the natives just left everything open. Here, they locked up before taking to the hills."

"Can you break down this door?" Dr. Fisher asked, trying to see through the smudge and grease-soiled window.

Charlie nodded and put the butt of his Franchi through the glass, then reached inside and turned the knob. The door pulled open to the tune of a clanging cowbell.

"Anybody home?" Donovan called out.

There was no reply.

"How do you feel about this?" he asked Charlie half seriously. Charlie answered by leading the group inside.

The smells that greeted them inside the store included sweet hibiscus as well as the musk of tropical fruits. A bowl of mangoes and breadfruit sat on the counter, next to a display of slightly stale *firi-firi*.

"How old does this look?" Donovan asked, crumbling one.

"A week . . . two," Dr. Fisher said, uncoiling the probe from the EnviroTester and pressing it into the flesh of a mango.

Charlie was about to bite into a *firi-firi* when the doctor slapped it out of his hand.

"Hey!" Charlie objected.

"Do you want to disappear too? Let me test this food."

"What have you got?" Donovan asked, watching the numbers flash across the small LCD on the EnviroTester. The ET unit, which was developed in the flood of biocybernetics patents that followed the Central American War, measured the spectra of various elements and determined anomalies. Cocaine crystals in shipments of saltwater taffy were the first anomaly the ET technology found.

"Strontium ninety-seven is not supposed to appear in mangoes, generally speaking," Dr. Fisher said.

"Radiation?"

"A particularly nasty kind. Buries itself in the food chain and appears in the damnedest spots. Cocaine products shipped from Central America following the war showed high elevations of strontium ninety-seven for years, if you recall."

Donovan didn't recall, but took the warning to heart.

"Don't eat anything," he said.

"Captain . . . we have to exist," Chief Smith said, one hand resting on his round stomach.

"We'll find something safe. Is anything safe?"

"Unknown till I test it," Dr. Fisher said. "These mangoes are contaminated. So is the breadfruit. The donut is okay."

"It's okay?" Smith asked.

"It's a little stale."

"Fine by me," Smith said, devouring two of them.

"Could strontium ninety-seven kill the population of Tahiti?"

"Not this fast, at least not by itself. There may be other factors. Let's keep looking."

6

They walked half a mile down the road in the direction of the market, and at the edge of it found a fruit stand. Like everything else it was locked up, in a fashion. Clear plastic drapes enclosed it and were zipped up, sealing in the odor of several tons of fruit that sat rotting in the steamy sun.

Dr. Fisher tested samples from all the bins, pausing only to slap away the flies and bees that swarmed inside and outside, everywhere.

"I'm getting strontium ninety-seven from the mangoes and barium one-eleven from the coconuts and breadfruit," he said. "This does not make a whole lot of sense." Peter was frowning, shaking his head.

"Why not?" Donovan asked.

"There must be some mechanism where one plant absorbs strontium and the other absorbs barium. When they're eaten together they make a lethal stew."

"That could kill off the population?"

"Unknown. But it can't have been pleasant for them. What really interests me is the absorption mechanism, though."

"This is hardly the time for pure science, Doctor."

"It relates to our predicament," Fisher said. "Something in those trees blocks the absorption of lethal fallout. All I have to do is isolate it. Maybe there's the beginning of an answer to our food problems down the road."

"What food problems?"

"Radioactive fruit," Alex answered for her brother. "If it happened on Tahiti, it could happen on all these islands."

"A sobering thought," Donovan said. "I need a drink while I think over this newest problem."

"I wouldn't trust the water, either. I have to test that, too," Fisher cautioned.

"I'll take it straight," Donovan growled.

Voices on the street announced the arrival of Chief Smith, Mr. Jennings and Charlie, who had been checking out the city's vital systems. Donovan went outside to greet them and Dr. Fisher followed.

"Well, this town is damned hot but the traffic lights work," Smith said, mopping his brow with a gigantic red bandanna.

"The infrastructure is intact?"

"Yeah, and the water flows good, too. Here, Doctor."

He handed over a rack of test tubes, water samples from strategic points in Papeete. Fisher began to test them right away.

"In short, everything works like it was designed. Only thing is, there ain't no one here to run it. I could put a few men at key spots and run the whole town. Don't know why—there's nobody here to live in it."

"Maybe we can move in ourselves—the colonists, I mean . . . once the food is clear to eat."

"And after the water is safe to drink, too," Fisher announced. "All those samples you gave me read high for strontium."

"So it's in the groundwater."

"And will have to be filtered out of the food and water."

"This may be Paradise, but only the bugs appear to be safe," Donovan said, angrily swatting a gigantic fly. "Why *are* there so many bugs, by the way?"

"There are always bugs in the tropics," Peter Fisher replied.

"Yeah, but this is crazy. These flies are like vampire bats. I've seen smaller vultures."

Alex said, "This is something I'll have to check the computer on. I don't know if so many bugs are normal, even for here."

"Do they sell bug spray around here?" Donovan asked.

"Why buy when you can steal?" Charlie asked. "There's a five-and-dime down the block that has lots of useful stuff."

"I take it you saw nobody."

Charlie shook his head. "I found a gun shop too. We can stock up on ammo. There's even bullets for your Colt."

"I'm not a thief, but we have to forage for provisions from here on. If radiation killed all these people, we might as well avail ourselves of their stuff."

"I didn't say they were dead," Dr. Fisher said. "Only missing."

"Missing where?"

"Ninety percent of this island is virgin," Alex added. "In the *fenua 'aihere*—the brushland—you can walk for miles without encountering a single soul."

"Now you're speaking Tahitian? Does everyone know more about this island than me? I'm the only one who wanted to come here."

"The language is French, more or less. And all you know about Tahiti is your middle-aged fantasies of nut-brown maidens."

"I got them from my father," Donovan retorted. "He married one."

"Well, forget it. You're taken. And besides, all the maidens have fled to the jungle. Why are we standing around bullshitting?"

"A commander getting reports from his men is not bullshitting. Mr. Jennings?"

"Yes, Captain?"

"Report on the island's communications."

"The harbormaster's radio is working. It's a primitive VHF but has a decent range, and is getting nothing. I found two police cars with functioning radios, but as is always the case these days, there's no one to call on them. Apart from the ship, of course. Mr. Percy reports no luck in his efforts to raise the international airport or anywhere else on Tahiti."

"Do you have everything you need, Doctor?" Donovan asked Fisher.

"More than enough. I just need to check a few water supplies at the actual faucet."

Jennings said, "Maybe we could test the water at the Royal Tahitian Yacht Club. Mr. Percy wants us to join him there. I believe he's liberated a small fleet."

"We'll go there now," Donovan said, adding, "Mr. Jennings, is Quinn's still open?"

"Yes!" the communications officer reported, beaming. "It's where it always was. The place is a little touristy for my taste, but that's not important."

"Now that tourists are no longer a factor. Let's go take a look at the fleet Mr. Percy has liberated for us."

The Royal Tahitian Yacht Club was a grand old wooden structure, built in 1890 as a haven for yachtsmen who were seeking escape from the rigors of Western civilization and, in many cases, American embezzlement laws.

Enough of them arrived for the latter reason to furnish the old mansion grandly, with six docks and an immense bar decorated with African ivory and the jawbones of whales. Framed maps detailed the history of oceanic navigation in the South Pacific, and a series of black-and-white photographs showed port development in Papeete as well as French nuclear tests in neighboring parts of the Pacific.

Next to the old brass cash register a cranky VHF, used in the old days to arrange the removal of drunken sailors from the bar to their boats, sputtered with radio traffic from *Liberator*, the club having been commandeered by Percy as temporary HQ for the Papeete expeditionary force.

"There is something extraordinarily odd about the way this operation gravitates to bars," Donovan observed, recalling finding Alex and her party of survivors HQ'd in a San Francisco tavern. "Not that many of us drink."

"I do," Chief Smith said, heading for what looked like a still-functioning beer cooler.

"The drinking lamp has *not* been lit," Donovan growled. "Go down in the basement and see if this dump will serve as HQ for us overnight. *Priscilla* is due in port tomorrow and we have to be ready."

"Sure thing." Grumbling, Smith trudged off.

Donovan addressed the young sailor who manned the radio: "Get Mr. Percy on the horn. Tell him to turn over the con to someone else and come ashore. I want to hear about this fleet he's liberated."

The "fleet" was majestic, if somewhat smaller than the Spanish Armada. It consisted of three ocean-ranging yachts of 50-, 70-, and 110-foot lengths, respectively, all of them fast and equipped with self-steering gear and automated systems designed for sailing long distances with a small crew. The smallest, a Design Forum 50, was sloop-rigged and could be sailed by two people while carrying ten passengers in comfort (or twenty passengers in mild discomfort).

Percy came ashore in one of the inflatables that had begun making shuttle runs to and from *Liberator* and handed over the bridge log, which officers had begun keeping on a microcomputer notepad in order to save irreplaceable paper. Donovan scrolled down the three pages of LCD notes, pausing now and again to comment or ask for more information.

"Have you tried listening on all available frequencies?" he asked.

Percy nodded. "We even called up the frequency used by flight mechanics at the airport and the one used by field supervisors on the plantations. There hasn't been a peep since we got here two hours ago."

"Have you been broadcasting on *Priscilla*'s frequency?"

"We got through to them on the scrambler half an hour ago. She is making good time with a persistent tail wind and will rendezvous with us at eleven hundred hours tomorrow. She had no contact with *Nemesis*."

"Good," Donovan said. "Maybe we've lost her for good."

"You don't really believe that."

"No, but I like to hope. What is the status of ship's stores—do we need anything?"

"The mess has prepared a shopping list," Percy said. "We need a lot."

"Let's hear it."

"Bread. Fresh water. Fruits and vegetables. Milk. Cereals. Just about everything you can name. And paper, lots of paper. Toilet paper is in special demand. And soap. Shall I go on?"

"No. In light of the extraordinary circumstances and unexplained absence of the regular population of this town, I have decided to put on my pirate's cap and loot it."

"Captain?"

"I have been through all the moral and legal ramifications, and am of the opinion that we have the right to take what we need. All the same, make a list of what you take and I'll leave an IOU just in case the town fathers come back and make an accounting."

"Does the doctor know what happened to them?" Percy asked.

"The leading theory is an as yet unexplained consequence of radiation psychosis; maybe a milder form than the white-shirts got."

"I'll send work parties ashore to collect what we need. I imagine the doctor wants medical supplies, too. There must be a few drugstores, even in Paradise."

"Consult the doctor first," Donovan said. "The fruits and vegetables in the markets have been irradiated. He'll tell you what you can and can't eat. Apart from that, I think the men will be safe. Have them come ashore in parties of fifteen and let them stay a shift each. Have them stick together in groups, though. I don't want anyone getting lost. And we still can't say the natives won't come back at any time."

"I'll get it organized," Percy replied. "Should the men be armed?"

"Yeah. Let's not take chances. The white-shirts may wear saris hereabouts but still be vicious. And tell the men to watch out for Mr. Jennings. He plans to renovate a bar in Papeete and may try to enlist help doing the work."

"Chief Smith has already volunteered," Percy said.

"It's good to be able to give the men shore leave," Donovan said. "We haven't had it since San Francisco, if you could call that adventure relaxing."

"Not as I remember it."

"Try to hold down the disreputable behavior. If need be, tell them that there's no women and the beer is stale. That should do it."

"I'll get right on it. And where will you be?"

"Right here at the club. I saw a small trimaran on pier three that I want to have a look at."

"For yourself, Captain?"

Donovan nodded. "Every captain is entitled to his personal boat."

"You're not going to sail to our new home in a twenty-seven foot boat," Alex said with undisguised horror.

"Why not?"

"Because these are shark-filled waters!"

"Where's your sense of adventure?"

"Back in the computer library. I read about adventure, Donovan, I don't do it."

"Is this the woman I remember as commander of the survivors in San Francisco? Packing a pistol and all that?"

"I've retired," she said. "I realize that my true value is in research and development. I'm hard at work designing a habitat for living, to be used once we find a new home."

"Make sure the one you design for you and me has a dock," Donovan insisted. "I intend to take the *Corsair* with us."

"You can't sail there. You have to steer the submarine."

"Hooper steers the submarine. I just sit behind him and play coach. Anyway, Mr. Jennings is an old sailor as well as a would-be bar owner. He's volunteered to sail her. And it won't take him long—the *Corsair* will do fifteen knots easily. We'll need a fast coastal sailboat once we're established on the island. What's the name of that island?"

"Espiritu. I don't know why you can't remember the name."

"Don't have to. My science officer remembers things for me. Hand me another Coke, would you?"

She pulled a bottle out of the Styrofoam cooler that had been set up on the porch of the Royal Tahitian Yacht Club and handed it to him, top off. He sipped it as he watched the first shore party come ashore from *Liberator*, looking like sailors always did when being turned loose on an island Paradise: both eager and apprehensive.

"I hope those guys don't get into too much trouble," he said.

"They shouldn't. Half of them are Ph.D.s, for God's sake, and the rest have advanced engineering degrees. This is hardly your stereotypical Navy crew. Probably they'll fix the water supply and detoxify the fruit."

Peter Fisher came out onto the porch carrying a stack of reports, and helped himself to a soda and a chair.

"I have some good news," he said, putting his feet up on another chair.

"Let's hear it."

"The contaminated fruit is no good and will have to be thrown out. But the stuff now growing on the trees is okay. The toxins apparently pass quickly through the surface soils and dissolve in the rock strata."

"Then the poisoning is transient!" Alex said, excitedly.

"It should be. The trees have already regained health and are producing edible fruit. The water supply will be okay once it's flushed. In short, there should be no problem in our living in the South Pacific indefinitely."

"Sensational!" Donovan said, and paused to radio the news to Percy on the ship and to Chief Smith, who commanded a party working to flush the city's water system. A moment later, a radio relay caused a whoop of delight to go up from the shore party. The word that it was safe to live in the islands spread quickly.

"Now all we have to do is find an island," Donovan said.

"We can't use this one," Dr. Fisher said. "At least not until I find out what happened to the population."

"We can't use it anyway. Tahiti is too well known. Enemies—and we have to assume there are some of them out there—will be able to find us. Espiritu is sounding better and better."

"And only a two-day sail for *Priscilla*. That means that the *Corsair* can make it in under a day."

"What's the *Corsair*?" Dr. Fisher asked.

"My boat," Donovan announced.

"I thought your boat was *Liberator*."

"That's my *ship*. I know that it's a fine distinction—boat and ship—but one you'll grow to understand. Carry on, Doctor."

"That means get back to work," Alex interpreted.

"I'll see if I can figure out what happened to the Tahitians." Dr. Fisher sniffed, returning to his lab setup inside the club.

"Come with me," Donovan said, taking Alex by the hand and leading her off the porch and in the direction of pier three.

The *Corsair* was three hulls wide and only twenty-seven feet long, but designed as a fast racer with ocean-crossing ability. Twenty-seven feet was indeed short for extended sailing in shark-infested waters, but she did have a cabin that slept four—two in comfort—and she was fast. One experienced man could sail her, and for two it was a breeze. Donovan figured she would be useful for running errands around their new home . . . going down the coast to look for something, or making short island hops.

Donovan helped Alex into the cockpit, which stretched ten feet from the transom to the companionway door. The cockpit was crammed with racing equipment—hydraulic boom vang and downhaul, self-tailing winches, and more navigation equipment than you could shake a stick at. The boat was equipped for a trans-Pacific crossing, with a fresh water distiller and solar panels on the cabin top that made electricity for the batteries. Everything about her said speed and ease of handling.

The companionway door swung open to reveal a

well-stocked cabin and a double-sized bunk. Donovan hooked his fingers under Alex's belt and pulled her to him.

"Welcome to the *Corsair*," he said. "I decided to keep the name."

"You have a thing about making love on boats," she said, not resisting at all.

"My mom and dad lived on one when I was a little kid. It used to rock me to sleep."

"That's my job now," Alex replied, whipping off her sweatshirt to free her breasts to the salt air.

At midnight the yacht club glowed merrily. The second shore party was reveling in the still tropical night. Their lights and those of *Liberator* out in the harbor were nearly all there were, apart from a three-quarter moon and the stars. The Southern Cross hung over a Papeete where only automatic streetlights glowed and the only men and woman stirring were submariners.

True, there were animals about. Dogs and cats came out from hiding with the evening. Lizards skittered about, as did land crabs, and after nightfall, the cries of birds filled the air. But people . . . there was no sign of them, and their absence grew more and more surreal as the night wore on.

Alex fell asleep early and slept like a rock. She was still dead to the world when the boat's chronometer struck eight bells for midnight. Donovan covered her with a cotton sheet and wandered up onto the dock, where the muted sound of music caught his ear.

Charlie sat on a mooring post listening to a compact disk player and staring out to sea. The player sat on the dock.

"Where'd you get that?" Donovan asked.

"I liberated it from a Tinito electronics shop a few blocks inland."

"Tinito?"

"Chinese. Don't worry—I left an IOU."

"I didn't see disk players on the shopping list of essential items."

"Music is essential. It's the one thing this crew is missing, other than women—and they're due tomorrow on *Priscilla*."

Donovan smiled. "The music rings a bell."

"It's the Stones' fortieth anniversary disk—a real oldie. Dad had one like it. I remember he used to sit on the bow of the *West Wind* and play it."

"Sounds good. Then again, I always did have old-fashioned tastes."

"Alex is asleep?"

"Yeah. I wish I could sleep like that. You could set off a bomb out here and she wouldn't wake up."

"Not that there's anything here to make noise. This crew ain't exactly a party crew. They have fun, but *really*."

"What are they doing?"

"There's a hot poker game raging up in the yacht club. At the same table where men have played poker for a hundred years. My sense is that nothing has changed."

Donovan offered a quizzical look.

"Since the war, I mean," his brother went on. "Everything and nothing have changed. We're still here, and we're still doing the stuff men have always done. Play poker, stand guard over sleeping women, and stare out to sea."

"Funny that we spend all our time at sea looking toward land, and when we get to land we turn around and look out to sea."

"Not exactly a profound or original thought, big brother," Charlie said.

"Like you said, nothing changes. Have the lookouts reported any sightings?"

"Not a damn thing. There's a couple of cats fighting over on the Boulevard Pomare and a couple of dogs barking at them, but other than that all is quiet."

"If the natives are around they ain't showing themselves. We haven't exactly kept a low profile." He nodded in the direction of *Liberator*'s mooring lights, which glowed across the harbor. "They must be dead."

"They're not dead," Charlie said authoritatively.

"How do you know?"

"I don't know. But they're out there in tne jungle."

"Doing what?"

"Wandering around. I don't know. It's just a feeling."

The disk player had come to the end of one side, and he paused to change it. Then from out of the silence came a crack of wood on wood and a splash.

"Oars!" he said. "Out there!" He pointed out to the darkness beyond the ghostly shadow of *Liberator*.

Donovan strained to see in the darkness but could find nothing. The sound persisted . . . a couple of cracks and splashes, then silence, then another sound of wood on wood.

That was followed by a shout from the watch officer on *Liberator* and the flicking on of a powerful spotlight that shot down from the topside bridge and cut a swath across the harbor.

Donovan and Charlie raced down the dock to where one of the inflatables was tied up, jumped inside, and revved up the engine. Soon Donovan was pushing the powerful outboard hard into the night while Charlie stood on the bow holding a Franchi.

Donovan whipped out his portable transceiver and spoke into it: "Captain to *Liberator* . . . we're heading out in the inflatable. What's going on?"

"One of the double-hulled canoes, Captain," was the reply. "It came fast out of the far shore of the harbor. There was no warning."

"Where is it now?"

"Dead ahead of you. Two hundred yards."

Charlie yelled back, "I can't see a thing."

"How come we didn't pick it up on sensors? What the hell was Communications doing?"

"I got it now! Slow down!"

Donovan eased off on the throttle and the outboard motor calmed to a gentle, purring roar as the small boat came off its plane and settled down into the still harbor water. At the same time, *Liberator*'s spotlight picked out the twin-hulled pirogue.

It lay in the darkness, ghostly in the spotlight, a solitary man standing in the starboard hull, a paddle in his hand. He wore a loincloth that seemed to have been fashioned out of khaki.

"What the hell?" Donovan said, to himself, really.

The intruder hefted the paddle as if it were a spear and threw it at the inflatable.

His aim was poor. The paddle splashed down four or five feet to one side of its target. Charlie raised the Franchi, then lowered the gun when he saw that the intruder had hurled his only weapon and was standing staring, an odd, lost look on his Polynesian face.

The sea gave forth an explosion of water and the pirogue rocked violently to one side as the dark dorsal fin of a gigantic shark smashed into it. The man tumbled into the water and disappeared immediately, torn in half by the four sharks that followed the first.

"Jesus fucking Christ!" Donovan yelled.

"Let's get outta here!" Charlie yelled back.

Donovan revved the engine back up and turned the inflatable hard to port.

His radio spoke: "Captain, sensors picking up sharks."

"We found them!" he shouted, and turned the boat toward *Liberator*.

The big shark that had overturned the pirogue turned on the inflatable, racing at it and striking it a glancing blow, rows of gleaming white teeth raking along the starboard side as Donovan turned the outboard away from it. Charlie shouted and a burst of automatic weapons fire tore into the creature. Two smaller sharks approached from the bow and he turned away from them too, the raft zigzagging toward *Liberator* amidst a sea of gleaming teeth and dorsal fins.

"There's sharks all over!" Charlie yelled, looking back as a wolf pack of small sharks attacked the blood scent on the big one he had shot up.

On *Liberator* men poured out onto the deck, Franchis and other guns at the ready. Three flares shot into the sky and illuminated the night. Another crew stood by the side, ready to take the inflatable on board.

In the growing light as the inflatable raced up to the hull of the submarine, Donovan could see the harbor almost carpeted with sharks. Their dorsals sliced the surface into a foam and their teeth slashed at the thin hull of the fleeing raft. Another big one zoomed in front of the inflatable and Donovan gunned the engine so that the raft skittered over it, the propeller cutting a row of slices into its back.

Donovan ran straight at the hull of *Liberator* in between two rows of automatic weapons fire as his men shot into the water to drive off the predators. White hands grabbed at the raft and hauled it aboard, Charlie and Donovan scrambled up onto the foredeck, hearing teeth gnash at the hull and weapons tear into angry black bodies.

Donovan turned to the sea and stared, astonished. As far as the spotlights could go, the water roiled with twisting sharks.

"Holy shit," Charlie said.

"All hands get below!" Donovan yelled. He chased them all down the hatches and scrambled to the bridge. "Emergency dive, straight down far enough to submerge the laser ports!"

"Aye, Captain."

He could feel the ship settling underneath him and watched the Cyclops display the depth. When the keel nearly touched the harbor bottom, *Liberator* stopped.

Donovan ordered, "Lasers on full power, three-hundred-and-sixty-degree dispersion ... repetitive fire!"

The blue-green lasers fired from hull-mounted ports fore and aft of the sail and swept the underwater horizon, using a design feature meant to clear mine fields. As the beams shot through the sea they tore up the marauding sharks, missing most but killing a few and wounding enough to turn the others upon them.

The firing lasted only ten seconds but the carnage continued for an hour. Eventually, *Liberator* resurfaced and men went up on deck to watch it. Before half an hour had passed, Papeete harbor stunk with blood and entrails.

Charlie said, "*Canis lupus lycaon.*"

"What?"

"Timber wolves. We knew there were sharks in these waters, but this is fuckin' insane."

"The same as in San Francisco," Donovan agreed. "Yeah, I get your point. Man blew himself up, and the beasts continue to inherit the earth. I didn't really think it would extend to the sea."

In reverse of the usual procedure—perhaps to suggest that in the wake of World War Three everything worked backwards—the big fish ate each other and the smaller fish snacked on the remains. Papeete harbor spent the night disguised as a feeding bin and by morning all were satisfied, except for a crewful of nervous Americans who had slept very little.

At noon of their second day in Tahiti, Donovan stood on the topside bridge and took reports. Ship's stores had been replenished with food and other supplies found in Papeete; the newly grown fruit was increasingly free of radiation; and after a full day in Paradise, none of the crew had gotten in trouble and the third shift was returning from shore leave.

Dr. Fisher reported: "None of the local inhabitants have been found, Captain. Apart from the man who tried to attack the ship."

"Any theories about him?"

"Reading the record of your exploits before I joined the crew, this does seem a repeat of what happened in Seattle and the Bering Strait."

"That's right. A white-shirt came at us in a speedboat and a Russian pilot strafed us in an antique plane with no bullets. It was a form of radiation psychosis."

"This too was, I imagine. He took a canoe and attempted to ram the ship, then used a paddle as a weapon. I don't want to be an alarmist, but I think we can continue to expect these attacks."

"But there's no sight of the rest of the natives," Donovan said.

"We can't see them, but they have to be there. In the interior, the jungle and the mountains. The price we pay for staying here is eternal vigilance."

"That's the price we pay for staying anywhere," Donovan said. "When we get to a less-populated island the danger will be proportionately less. What is the word from *Priscilla*?"

"Radar reports her four miles out and making six knots under full sail," Jennings reported. "Two inflatables have gone out to meet her and escort her into the harbor."

"Considering the danger, I want the colonists on the way to Espiritu within twenty-four hours," Donovan said.

"What about the other two islands?" Alex asked.

"We'll check them out when we have time. Right now we have to turn about that schooner and get it to Espiritu. I can't let a boatload of colonists wander around unprotected in Papeete, especially since I don't know when the natives are going to hop into canoes and attack. No, *Priscilla* will have to reprovision and sail on."

"That island is emerging as our best bet," Alex said. "Documents located in the yacht club reaffirm our information that it's remote—well out of the normal trade routes—but well able to support up to a thousand colonists."

"We'll escort her to Espiritu and start setting up camp. If all we have to do is blast a harbor, it should be no problem."

Charlie was helping out the bridge watch, and announced, in a voice proud and lyrical, "Sail ho! Topsail schooner at the harbor mouth, escorted by two dinghies."

"Sail ho?" Donovan said, with a smile.

"Aye, Captain."

"Three months to sail from San Francisco Bay to Tahiti. I think Captain Cook moved faster. The important thing is they got here."

Jennings said, "I have *Priscilla* on the radio, Captain. She wants instructions."

"Have her raft up with us so Dr. Fisher can check the colonists. I want shore leave for all those who check out. We'll use the yacht club and the hotel across the street as temporary housing. Listen to me on this: there are to be no colonists wandering about Papeete. Groups of ten only, and two armed guards with each party. No freelance looting, please. We'll provide everything they need. I'll tell them about Espiritu. Alex will draw up new charts for the skippers who will be sailing *Priscilla* and the other sailboats to Espiritu tomorrow."

The wooden schooner made the turn into the channel and sailed up it, her sharply defined bow cutting through clean water that only hours before was the scene of tropical carnage. The captain had dressed ship for the landfall—pennants of every color and configuration flew from her halyards, and a large bat-shaped kite trailed behind at the end of a long tether. Air horns on *Priscilla* and the inflatables blared a greeting that was returned from the newly created fleet tied up at the yacht club. After the war and three long months of struggle, the first group of nuclear survivors had arrived in their new world.

Donovan, Alex, and Charlie went out onto the foredeck, and Donovan caught the first line tossed from the schooner. As the old wooden boat drew alongside the ultramodern submarine, Donovan felt the continuity of the old and the new united in creating a new world amidst the ashes of the dead one. In this island Paradise a new Eden would evolve, with new children and hope for the future. From its shores, *Liberator* and, eventually, other ships, would venture out on missions of rescue to the rest of the world.

As the several dozen colonists received medical okays and were ferried to shore, there to try out land legs made shaky by months at sea, Donovan and his officers conferred with the captain of *Priscilla* and the leaders of the colonists and agreed. The schooner, renamed *Mayflower II*, would depart the next day for Espiritu, where a new world would have its origin. There would be no delay. They would get on with the task of creating the future.

Liberator's second night in Papeete was deadly slow. Donovan sat on the bow of the submarine looking once again out to sea while the disk player, borrowed from Charlie, played Duke Ellington. The yacht club was ablaze with lights, as was a five-block chunk of Papeete surrounding it, the better to ward off evil spirits or deranged natives, whichever came first.

The harbor too was illuminated. Spotlights from *Liberator* and the four yachts in the new fleet swept the waters, guarding against pirogues with phantom figures. *Mayflower II* was lit up like a Christmas crèche and lookouts sat in the ratlines, taking advantage of the newly arrived high vantage point. And *Liberator*'s sensors swept the underwater, just in case the bizarre phenomenon that had come to be called the uprising of the beasts again appeared.

No one slept very much, and all yearned for 1200 hours, when the fleet would weigh anchor for Espiritu.

Donovan was listening to Billie Holiday sing *God Bless the Child* when he heard footfalls on the deck and looked over his shoulder to see Jennings hurrying up, a tape player in his hand.

"You got to hear this, Captain," he said excitedly.

Donovan shut off the disk player.

"What have you got?"

"A radio message on the amateur frequency. Damned if I didn't pick up a ham radio operator in New York."

"New York?" Donovan said excitedly, thinking of his presumed-dead parents.

"In Sheepshead Bay. Do you know where that is?"

"Yeah, it's a small fishing port in the nether portion of Brooklyn. My dad took me on a party boat out of there once. I caught a five-pound fluke and won the kitty. What did the guy say?"

Jennings flicked on the recorder. An electronically augmented voice said, "Calling CQ from Sheepshead Bay in New York City. Calling for anyone who can respond. We are..."

"Here it starts to break up," Jennings said.

"...alive... The city... gone... Manhattan... is... We are alone among the ruins. Can't get far from the ocean. 'The crazies rule the inland.'"

Jennings said, "He repeats that phrase several times: 'The crazies rule the inland.'" He played it for the captain to hear.

The fragment concluded: "Holding out. Calling for help. Batteries low. Is there anyone listening? I have battery power one more hour."

"That's all of it," Jennings said.

"'Can't get far from the ocean. The crazies rule the inland,'" Donovan said numbly.

"There must be white-shirts in New York, too."

"They're everywhere," Donovan said. "According to the computer model, radiation psychosis is on all the continental land masses. This message confirms it. Only the coastal zones are safe, and only pockets of civilization remain. Did you return the call?"

"No, Captain. Your orders are to avoid use of radio in order to avoid detection by *Nemesis*."

"Break radio silence. Call this man and tell him we're on our way and will be there in..." Donovan did some fast calculating. "Two weeks."

"How will we get there?" Jennings said, incredulously.

"Through the Panama Canal."

"If it's still there."

"There's only one way to find out. Look, Jennings, this message tells us that there are survivors on the East Coast."

"The Panama Canal was a prime target for nuclear

attack. It would have been wiped out in the war."

"New York was a prime target too, and it's still there. Part of the coast, anyway."

Donovan looked at his watch.

"Get Mr. Percy and Chief Smith out of the sack and have them meet me on the bridge. We have a change of plans."

"New York is *still there*?" Percy exclaimed.

"A small part of it. The point is that we have a new group of survivors to rescue. There are white-shirts on the East Coast, too."

"How many?" Smith asked.

"Hard to tell. But if there are some in a coastal area of New York City, a prime target, there could be pockets of survivors up and down the East Coast. We have to go there and check it out."

"What about Espiritu?" Percy asked.

"The colonists made it all the way across the Pacific on their own. They can sail two more days to Espiritu. Besides, they'll be protected. Mr. Jennings has agreed to ride shotgun."

"Who'll lead them?"

"I will," Alex said, taking her place by the captain's side.

"You're not coming with us to New York?"

"My main job here is to find a site for our new home and supervise the building of it," she said.

"Jennings is a fine sailor and also dedicated to building a life in the South Pacific," Donovan continued.

"I'm not a bad shot, either," Jennings cried out from his position at the communications console.

"My brother is a communications specialist. He can take over Mr. Jennings's duties on board *Liberator*," Donovan said.

"I'm checked out on communications," Hooper volunteered. "I can back him up."

"We'll have to do each other's jobs occasionally from now on," Donovan said. "Including mine. No one has a monopoly anymore."

"And if we can't make it through the canal?" Percy asked.

"We'll go around the Horn. It will take longer, but there's work to be done. If part of New York survived, maybe part of Washington did as well."

"We can pick up our paychecks," Charlie said.

"We sail at twelve hundred hours," Donovan concluded. "We'll see the fleet into open water, then turn east for Panama."

The fleet—*Liberator*, the schooner, and the four sailboats—left Papeete promptly at noon. There had been no untoward acts during the night: no more attacks, either by shark or by native, and neither colonist nor crew member got out of hand, even with a whole town to themselves. Mr. Jennings had no luck in raising the ham radio operator in Sheepshead Bay. If the man got *Liberator*'s message, his batteries were too low for him to reply. Or so they could hope. The only way to know was to go there.

At 1300 hours on a glorious South Pacific day, the fleet turned to the southwest for the final plunge to Espiritu and what everyone agreed would be their best possible future. Alex and Jennings led in the trimaran and the other boats trailed along in a ragtag fleet that soon stretched across ten miles of sea.

Donovan watched as the boats sailed into the horizon and over it. Alex and he said their farewells in the wee hours of the night and welcomed the dawn fast asleep in each other's arms. Several other officers also spent the night with colonists they had befriended in San Francisco. Donovan was hardly the only one to feel a profound sense of separation when the wind-powered fleet sailed on to the promised land without them.

He ordered a dive to 700 feet, then took a last look at

the sun before pulling the hatch shut behind him. With the sea clear of everything but dolphins and sharks and a good head of steam up in the engines, Donovan had Hooper set course for Panama and increased speed to flank.

The course took *Liberator* through the Tuamotu Group of islands and across the belly of the Pacific 6,500 miles to Panama, passing north of the Galapagos and entering Central American waters on the morning of the sixth day.

Donovan surfaced while steaming due north, lining up with the shipping lane approach to the canal, which ran from southeast on the Pacific side northwest to the Caribbean. *Liberator* returned to the surface halfway between Punta Mala on the Azeuro Peninsula and Jaque, a town a few miles up the coast from the border with Colombia. The Golfo de Panamá was strangely alive, with wave and current action completely out of synch with computer projections and Donovan's experience.

"What the hell is this wave action about?" he said, mostly to himself, as his other officers joined him on the topside bridge.

"I don't know," Charlie said. "But I made a sweep of the UHF and VHF bands and got nothing. Passive radar shows no contacts. Active radar shows only the expected shore features. Of course, we're a bit far out to get a clear shot of the canal approach markers."

"What about the channel markers?"

"The computer is reading them perfectly. We're right in the middle of the inbound shipping channel."

Shortly after the canal reverted to American control at the outbreak of the Central American War, the Corps of Engineers placed laser channel markers, similar to those that guided ships into American harbors, in the approaches to the canal. American naval ships and escorts were then able to ride the computer track into and out of the canal, speeding things up and minimizing the chance of collision.

"The computer cannot account for these currents," Charlie concluded.

"I've never seen them either," Percy added. "And I've been through the canal half a dozen times."

Though there was little wind, only a five-knot breeze from the northeast, the waves were running at six feet and ragged, more appropriate to a thirty-knot wind. And a three-knot current swept up from the southwest, moving from the Pacific into the Golfo de Panamá and towards the canal.

As the coastline rose from behind the horizon and laid itself bare to radar, Charlie announced, "Reading the land from Vacamonte Point to Panama City, I get the usual topographic features. We're too far out to read buildings."

"What about the radar reflectors at the canal entrance?" Donovan asked.

"I don't read them. Of the eight reflectors noted on the chart, not one remains."

"And the gas storage tanks starboard of the canal entrance?"

"We're too far out. I can tell you this, though: these inner waters are damned clear. There's *nothing on them*. Usually in the approaches to a major harbor facility there's lots of navigational aids that reflect radar. I'm getting nothing. No markers or buoys at all."

"Are they all blown away?"

"Yeah, unless this giant hand came out of the sky and plucked them from the bay bottom."

Newly arrived on the bridge, Dr. Fisher said, "On that score, I'm getting residual radiation that fits the Seattle model."

"Panama is as hot as Seattle?"

"Let me put it this way: it's as hot as Seattle is *now*, three months after the war. It's cooled off a lot, but still nowhere I'd plan to settle down and raise kids. Everyone in this town is doomed, assuming there's anyone left alive."

"The canal *was* listed as a primary target," Donovan said. "Apparently, whoever nuked it was a good shot.

Dammit, I wish we knew who was responsible for this war."

"Does it matter?" Fisher asked.

"Only to the historically curious," Donovan allowed. "But that includes me."

"I'll make a more accurate radiation count after we get inland. But there's no doubt that exposure outside the ship's hull will have to be limited."

"What the *hell* is this water doing?" Donovan asked as an especially strong cross-flow pushed *Liberator*'s bow momentarily off course.

After another fifteen minutes, the ship nosed closer to land and, as land features grew up from the horizon, the radar sweeps grew weirder. "Reading the canal entrance now," Charlie said. "You're not gonna believe this."

"What?"

"The canal is five miles wide at the entrance, narrowing to three miles wide once you get five miles inland and a mile across at ten miles in."

"That's not right. No way is that right."

"Check it yourself," Charlie said, letting his brother have a look into the topside radar display.

Donovan stared at it for a long moment, then gave way to Percy.

"I'll be damned."

"We all will."

"Explanation?" Donovan asked. "The last time I passed through, it was a hundred and fifty yards wide."

"Wave action," Charlie said. "Erosion."

"From this current?"

"You got it. My guess is that the canal locks were blown away in the nuclear attack, making the Panama Canal one fuck of a lot wider and removing all barriers to Pacific water flooding into the Atlantic."

"Accounting for the strange currents," Percy said.

Donovan added, "The canal is, in essence, a gigantic funnel draining the Pacific. It won't *drain* it completely, just make for the world's strongest river current. I don't know if we'll be able to navigate it."

"Not with a tail current we won't," Percy said. "A five-knot current fucks up the ship's steering by fouling the rudder hydrodynamics. A ten-knot or greater current will completely destabilize the ship. Our only hope would be to shoot through the canal like a rocket and pray we don't hit anything."

"That is *not* what I have in mind for my ship," Donovan said tersely.

"I ain't lookin' forward to it either," Charlie replied, studying the topside bridge display one more time. "The width does seem to stabilize at a mile after it gets inshore."

"Can you run a computer simulation of what it would be like to navigate the canal in its current condition?" Donovan asked.

"I can try."

"Try?"

"The real computer expert is back in the Society Islands, lookin' for a place to build huts," Charlie replied.

According to plan, the trimaran made it to Espiritu a good ten hours ahead of *Mayflower II*, but as fate would have it, it arrived in the middle of the night.

In a light breeze she spent six hours running east and west along the inhabitable coast, looking for campfires and other signs of human activity. With night vision binoculars borrowed from *Liberator*, Jennings found a cluster of pirogues right where satellite photos placed the island's only settlement. But there were no lights and no other signs of life apart from luminescent plankton and flying fish that burst from the sea all around the sailboat.

In the breaking dawn, Espiritu looked like a gigantic figure eight that had been laid on its side. It was ten miles long and four miles wide, with the western half of the island being taken up by the active volcano. It rose 2,000 feet above the Pacific and oozed smoke with a kind of gentle menace. Around its base was a dense tropical jungle that extended in all directions but north, where there was a sheer cliff.

The eastern end of the island was a typical South Pacific atoll—a circle of volcanic rock and coral surrounding the caldera of an older, extinct volcano.

The land was narrow, only a half mile wide at one point and no more than a mile wide anywhere, and broken in three places where the sea came in at high tide and during storms.

Jennings took the trimaran around to the northeast side of the ring, where he found a break that was deep enough for them to get through the three concentric layers of coral.

On the shore was a broad strip of beach on which were stored eight native canoes, both single and double-hulled pirogues. A similar beach was on the south side of the island, where the coral ring was attached to the mountainous western end.

"Oh, brave new world," Alex said, looking in at the dense stand of tropical vegetation.

"Want to go ashore?" Jennings asked, strapping on his Franchi and an extra belt of ammunition.

"My computer projection of conditions inside the canal shows that we can survive passage through it," Charlie announced, rather proudly.

"Survive?" Donovan asked.

"It's the best I can do. The computer says that we can turn around at any point up to where the canal narrows to a mile."

"What happens after that?"

"After that we got a fifteen-knot current or stronger smacking us in the tail."

"We can't turn around in that," Chief Smith said. "Not in the width of a mile, anyway. We'd get broadside to the current and be dragged sideways. A hard turn to port would only result in an uncontrolled drift to starboard."

"Which would make us prey to whatever the current wants to push us into," Donovan said.

"Which can't be much," Charlie went on. "That water is really tearing through that canal. There's not much holding it back. The current could shoot us right through."

"Can't take the chance. There could be things we can't see . . . sunken wrecks, shallow water, landslides. The canal always had problems with landslides."

"I agree with the captain," Percy said.

"From the radar, I can see that the canal goes inland for ten miles before narrowing to one mile in diameter," Charlie said. "You guys know this ship better than me . . . can we go in nine miles and then turn back if things get too hairy?"

"Can we?" Donovan asked the chief.

"We can go in *seven* miles and *then* start our turn," he replied.

"That will give us a better picture of what lies ahead," Donovan said. "If the way looks clear we can continue on. If it's too hairy we can turn back."

"Before we're swept against a submerged object or one of the canal banks and crushed," Smith warned.

"Damn. This ship was *not* designed to shoot the rapids. When I decided to embark upon a program of global rescue I knew we'd have to improvise, but this is ridiculous."

"Amen, brother," Charlie added.

"One thing's for sure—we'll have to come and go through this canal a lot in the future. We may as well try it now."

"I suggest we vote," Smith said. "The men should know what the dangers are."

"Agreed," Donovan said. "Put pictures of the canal entrance up on shipwide video along with the radar screen and the computer data. I'd like opinions from everyone."

"Aye, Captain," Percy said.

The canal entrance loomed on the near horizon, a gaping maw that appeared to be sucking the whole Pacific Ocean into it. The current that was merely an oddity when they were in the middle of the Golfo de Panamá had become a massive force, twisting and churning and dragging tree trunks as well as ocean bottom into the canal. The navigation markers that were absent when Charlie did his first radar scan must have been among the first objects sucked in when a brace of hundred-megaton nuclear explosions ripped the old canal, widening it into a torrential strait.

"I feel like Byron trying to swim the Dardanelles," Donovan said.

"He made it, didn't he?" Charlie replied.

* * *

Jennings and Alex rolled up the legs of their jeans and walked the short distance to the beach.

The water was crystalline, like that in travel ads. Small fish flitted over a sandy bottom dotted with exotic shells and mother-of-pearl. The beach was narrow—all the northern beaches were narrow. Only 100 feet from the high-water mark it disappeared into a forest of towering palm and ground-hugging broad-leafed tropical shrubs. A narrow trail came out of the jungle and broadened into a 50-foot-wide space where the ground had been cleared and turned into a dry dock for native pirogues, both single and twin-hulled.

They stood on the beach for a long moment, looking around, before Alex pronounced, "Nobody's home."

"Doesn't look that way. Follow me."

He led the way to the clearing, then fell to his knees and examined the soil and the canoes.

"This land hasn't been disturbed in months," he said.

"What do you mean?"

"These seedlings are at least two months old. This one's a baby hibiscus. Look at it."

Alex found that he was right. The ground was covered with seedling plants, all at least two months old. The pirogues hadn't been moved in that long, though they had been slightly before that. Old drag marks in the sand hadn't entirely been worn away by the wind and rain.

Jennings got back to his feet. "Even the trail is starting to grow plants. Like you said, no one's home."

"Where have they gone?"

"The same place the natives of Tahiti went. Unknown."

Alex unpacked her EnviroTester and made tests of air, sand, and leaves.

"The air is perfect," she announced. "The sand is good down to six inches. Below that it shows traces of strontium ninety-seven."

"The radiation is being diluted by rainwater."

"Right. It's also being eliminated by the food chain. It's found in the older leaves, but not in the new growth. We have the same conditions here as in Tahiti."

"Which means we can survive," Jennings said.

"Yeah. I think we can do well."

The yawning gap that was once the Pacific entrance to the Panama Canal beckoned from a distance of only three miles. That close it looked as wide as the horizon itself, and made up of land that had been twice decimated—by nuclear holocaust and then by the torrent of water pouring through. Only the shells of buildings remained, the taller ones.

Everything bigger than three stories was stripped like an elm in a hurricane, a charred side to the north, facing central Panama along the route of the canal. The devastation was very much like that in San Francisco—selective, with some areas of the countryside surviving the blast relatively intact.

Curiously, it was worst on the northern side of the canal, which was the least developed. Almost nothing remained but rubble, and that side was the most eroded by the raging water.

From three miles out and faced with being drawn into a funnel that led to the unknown, the crew of *Liberator* voted to go ahead.

"Turbines at full power, engines ahead full," Donovan ordered, then gripped the splash rail as the submarine drove forward into the funnel.

Donovan had cleared the topside bridge of all but Percy and himself, with the first officer handling communication down to the helm and engine room. Both of them had their safety harnesses hooked securely to the splash rail. It promised to be a wet and bumpy ride, akin to smashing through North Atlantic swells during a March storm.

Of all the things Donovan had seen, this was the largest example of the war's earth-shattering consequences. The explosions that hit the Panama Canal set off an incredible series of events. One warhead must have detonated between Diablo Heights and Pedro Miguel near the Pacific end, melting down the Miraflores locks and blasting canal mechanisms and bulkheads along a five-mile stretch. The second warhead had to have struck over the Atlantic end of the canal, devastating the locks at Gatun.

The effect was to uncork the Pacific Ocean, which poured through by the billions of gallons, ripping up all the structures built by man and widening the canal until it reached its natural, topographically defined banks. Gatun Lake, always the biggest body of water along the canal route, became a vast tidal whirlpool, twice its old depth and ruled by swirling currents that only reluctantly poured into a second funnel—near the remains of Gatun—and then emptied into the Atlantic.

Liberator entered the funnel near the ruins of the old Fort Amador, south of Panama City, making twenty knots and accelerating, mostly due to the increased current.

"Current reads five knots," Percy called out, as the submarine raced by the shoreside sight of wrecked barracks that a few months ago were three miles inland.

"Read the bottom for me," Donovan replied, involuntarily holding on to the splash rail.

"The channel markers are swept away. The helmsman is following the deep channel carved out by the current, as you ordered."

"Maybe we *can* shoot the rapids. How does sonar read the bottom?"

"The channel is good as far ahead as we can read—three miles on this straightaway."

"That's not much room to stop or turn around in if sonar sees an obstruction," Donovan said.

"No it isn't. Our only hope is that the current was strong enough to have already swept away everything big enough to damage us."

"Do we have enough room to turn?"

"There's plenty of water now. Ask me again in three miles."

With the current behind it accelerating to seven and then ten knots, and the surrounding terrain largely devastated, *Liberator* raced deep into the heart of the Panamanian isthmus. The land flew by too quickly for Donovan to take much notice of details, but he could see that nothing much remained of the old canal and countryside. When the newly cut canal narrowed to a mile and the current jumped to an unheard-of fifteen knots, *Liberator* was going faster than thirty-five knots on the surface and water cascaded over the bow as wave after wave broke over the topside bridge.

Donovan and Percy held on for dear life, feeling very much like old-time whalers on a Nantucket sleighride. Donovan did look a bit like Ahab riding the whale, considering *Liberator*'s porpoise-back topside hull shape.

"I'd give a year's pay for a bigger conning tower," he shouted at Percy, who couldn't make out the words and only nodded as a courtesy and to get the water off his face.

"The channel is deep and wide as far ahead as sonar can scan," Percy shouted. "I think we can make it."

"To where?" Donovan shouted back.

The coral ring of east Espiritu enclosed a saltwater lake or cove that was, for all purposes, bottomless.

Formed in the caldera of the extinct volcano, it was protected from sharks and other large sea animals by the coral and volcanic rock surrounding it. A thriving colony of food fish lived in the cove, so rich a resource of ocean life that nearly all the native fishing was done within it. Nets hung drying in trees along the western cove.

With the Franchi sweeping the lush underbrush from one side of the trail to the other, Jennings and Alex prowled cautiously inland. As they walked, the birds alerted one another and then fell silent as they walked by, and lizards froze in their tracks to let the intruders pass.

"All is as it should be," Jennings said.

"Yeah, this is damned normal. Except the people are gone."

He looked down at the trail. "No one has walked here in months. Look at how these plants crush beneath our feet. It's as if the natives dried up and blew away, leaving all their worldly possessions to us."

"They disappeared on Tahiti."

"Yeah, but there are more places for them to get lost in there. Here there's just the volcano."

"You don't think . . ."

"That they jumped inside? No, but it makes more sense than their drying up and blowing away," Jennings said.

"Where does this left-hand trail go?" Alex asked, eyeballing a fork in the path the left branch of which led off to the east.

"The cove, I imagine. It's only a hundred yards away."

"Let's check it out."

The cove was like a miracle to them. Only three miles across and flat as a mirror, it was apparent even from the shore that it was teeming with fish. Nets were hung everywhere on their side of the cove, and another fleet of canoes waited on the beach for someone to claim and use them.

"This is incredible," Jennings said. "We can fish right here without risking sharks."

"A naturally protected marine ecosystem with an abundant supply of fish," Alex agreed. "I have read of islands like this. There are several in the Marshalls and another couple in the Marianas. If this cove proves as abundant as it looks, we can live here forever."

Jennings walked to one of the twin-hulled pirogues and kicked it. "As soon as the colonists get here we can launch the Tahitian navy."

"The what?"

"Tahitian navy. That's the captain's term for natives in canoes."

"That's his sense of humor all right," she noted, smiling despite herself. "I wonder how he's doing in Panama."

The wreckage of Panama City flew by like the walls of a tunnel as seen from a speeding train.

Donovan saw everything and nothing. What stuck out from the blur were wrecked, stark spires like burned Christmas trees where apartment houses and office buildings used to be.

The once-narrow canal had been widened to a strait, one where the rampaging waters had cut new banks from the decimated walls of urban structures. But the channel held wide and deep, and *Liberator*'s engines kept the ship speeding at twenty knots, a speed that allowed Hooper to steer well enough despite the fifteen-knot current behind him.

Once through the rubble of the old Miraflores locks and Diablo Heights, where through-hull radiation monitors leapt off the scale during the passage, *Liberator* found herself twenty miles inland and in a river suddenly narrowing.

As abruptly as it had narrowed, the strait widened. The current reversed its acceleration down through ten and five knots before settling down and pouring into a mammoth lake that had been carved out of the interior of the narrow country by backflow from congestion on the Atlantic side.

As the current slackened, *Liberator* throttled back and cruised into the lake, which was so wide that, from the middle, it was impossible to see to any shore. It had been a chaotic ride inland, but the ship and crew survived with no injuries worse than a few bruises, the result of being tossed into bulkheads as the ship was shaken by the current.

"Topside bridge officers on deck," Donovan ordered, and within seconds lookouts and other personnel had joined him.

The submarine was cruising north, in the general direction of the Atlantic side of the canal.

"This has got to be Gatun Lake," Charlie said, calling up a picture of the old lake on his topside bridge monitor.

"Gatun Lake was never the size of Lake Superior," Donovan remarked.

"Things have changed. This is Gatun Lake, all right. I'm even reading a few channel markers on the bottom. But it's twice the size and got more currents. Preliminary analysis shows a vast whirlpool."

"Whirlpool? A dangerous one?"

"Not to us. The computer theorizes a clockwise whirlpool moving at three knots and discharging into the Atlantic past some kind of obstruction."

"The obstruction would account for the size of this lake," Percy said. "A sudden shallowing on the Atlantic end of the canal would produce a damlike effect."

"Turning Gatun Lake into a reservoir," Donovan said. "Can we get past this obstruction into the Atlantic?"

"We won't know until we see it," Percy said.

"Take us there, one-quarter speed."

"Course has been set for the locks at Gatun," he replied after a minute, adding, "Or what's left of them."

"Charlie, what do sensors say about this lake?"

"I read fifty feet of water under the keel. This is apparently the old channel, with maybe a little extra water. The lake shallows progressively to port and starboard. We can't go more than ten miles either to the east or west without running out of water."

"So we're stuck with the old channel and ten miles each side. That's not too bad. What about the islands in the lake?"

"All under water, from what I can tell. Most of them were marshes anyway. My guess is that the damming effect added twenty feet of water to the old lake."

Donovan said, "This is getting to be a dumb question, but are we alone? Is there anything on the airwaves?"

"Not so much as a peep. No radio. No TV. No radar. The electromagnetic spectrum is truly a vast wasteland."

As *Liberator* sailed north, the horizon grew darker and larger and soon grew into a strip of land that ran nonstop from west to east. Finally, Charlie announced, "Ten miles to Gatun, Captain, or what used to be there."

"What's there now?" Donovan asked, straining to see through his binoculars.

"Shoreline with no features. Blasted flat as a beach. In fact, a beach is pretty much what it is. White crystalline sand with nothing on it taller than three feet."

As the ship got closer to what was supposed to be the portal to the Atlantic, the assessment was repeated and clarified.

"Gatun is mostly flatlands, with one exception—where this water is going."

"I can see what looks like breakers on a windward shore," Donovan said.

"I analyzed information from sonar, lasers and radar, and got bad news."

"Let's hear it."

"The wall of water that we rode in here on has made this lake and now is spilling into the Atlantic over a dam."

"What?" Donovan asked.

"Something—I suppose a really big thermonuclear detonation—blasted up a wall of sand hundreds of yards thick at this end of what used to be Gatun locks. The water is spilling over it and into the Atlantic. Maybe there is and maybe there isn't a really big crater on the other side of that wall. My point is there ain't no way we're getting over it in this boat."

"Are you sure of this?"

"I checked the data, Captain," Percy said. "Your brother is right."

Liberator moved in fast on the wall, and soon Donovan could confirm the conclusion for himself. They were confronted with a mammoth earthen dam that blocked all hope—for the immediate future—of getting through into the Atlantic.

"You're right. We ain't gettin' through that."

"We could go ashore and look it over, Captain," Percy said. "If it isn't that thick we could blast it with torpedoes. Of course, we need a safe anchorage, and I don't see one in this maelstrom."

"Me either," Donovan said gloomily, looking dejectedly at the Niagara-like wall of water ahead of the ship.

Charlie added, "Water is shallowing fast, Captain. We only have another two miles of water before running aground."

"Helm hard to starboard. Have Mr. Hooper take us back to the middle of the lake. Let's find a place to anchor and plan our next move."

The native settlement on Espiritu lay up another trail from the beach and was in the middle of the island, near the juncture of the ring-shaped east from the volcanic west.

All the trails encountered by Jennings and Alex had several months of new growth on them. No human foot or hand had disturbed them, and the trappings of civilization had simply been abandoned, left and forgotten in the jungle.

The settlement lay on a flat area beneath a canopy of palms. The huts were classic South Pacific—circular, with conical, pandanus roofs, and arranged in no particular order amidst a spectacular display of breadfruit, mango, hibiscus, and frangipani. A stone *marae*, an ancient sacrificial altar, stood in a hallowed spot where the noon sun shone straight down on it between three immense palms the tops of which had been carefully pruned to admit the shafts of light.

"Primitive religious beliefs," Alex noted, a bit uneasily.

She unpacked her EnviroTester and stuck the probes into mangoes and breadfruit that Jennings had just plucked from nearby trees. Within seconds, a report flashed on the LCD.

"Both are as pure as the driven snow," Alex said happily.

"There's no strontium ninety-seven?"

"There's no nothin'. Plenty of vitamins. I think we found a home."

"And no natives, either," Jennings said. "The baby palms are growing just as fast in the village as on the trails. Wherever the people got to, they got there fast."

"It's easier to imagine five hundred natives disappearing than ten thousand Tahitians. Still, I'd like to know where they went."

"Isn't it enough to be glad they're not here?" Jennings said. "I think I'll call the fleet and check on its progress."

"Might as well. This place may be deserted, but that altar gives me the creeps. I wouldn't mind company."

Jennings's enhanced-range pocket UHF could reach ships twenty miles away at sea level, and forty miles away when raised to an elevation of 100 feet, the approximate height above sea level of the village.

"Jennings to *Mayflower II*. Do you copy?"

"Five-by, Jennings. Are you on the island?"

"Affirmative. We are in the promised land and you are welcome to join us."

Jennings smiled as a chorus of whoops and yells came over the airwaves. "We are in the promised land" was the code message indicating that Espiritu had checked out and the colonists were cleared to land.

"We're on our way, Jennings," was the eventual reply.

"What's your ETA?"

"Fifteen hundred hours to the landfall you described on the northeast coast."

"We'll be waiting to guide you through the shoals. It looks like a good anchorage."

"My people are coming home," Alex said happily.

"And what a long, strange trip it's been," Jennings agreed.

Liberator steamed around Gatun Lake for two hours, recording currents and depths and videotaping everything in sight for later analysis.

As daylight ebbed and there loomed no place to hide, Donovan ordered the ship into an old channel on the south side of the lake. That channel was once used for cargo layovers but was closed to regular traffic during the second administration of President-for-Life Romanus, who tore down the old port of Frijoles and, in its place, erected Ciudad Romanus in celebration of his return from exile.

The Central American War left the region bloodied but unbowed, and actually served to weed out the less stable elements in the global drug trade. While a few of the bigger Colombia drug barons were vaporized in the war, others took their place following that war's inconclusive end. They paid to reestablish the Romanus regime and, in return, he built Ciudad Romanus as a high-tech, heavily armored cocaine and marijuana depot.

Off-limits to gringos and their traffic under the terms of the Panama Canal Treaty of 1996, Ciudad Romanus was never visited except by its own traffic. All charts showed it as a forbidden city, and the old channel was off-limits to traffic.

"This place could have its uses," Donovan said as *Liberator* steamed slowly up the channel to the forbidden city.

"If it's still there," Percy replied.

"It should be. Romanus was scared by the damage done to the Colombia coke fields and, consequently, built his palace city to be as blast- and radiation-proof as possible. If it didn't take a direct hit, large parts of it could still be standing. There could be survivors."

Charlie said, "Radar contact with the city, Captain. The basic outline is still there."

"Distance?"

"Five miles."

"Becoming visible through the fog now," Percy said, handing binoculars to Donovan.

The captain peered with clear disdain at Ciudad Romanus, the outlines of which were appearing lit by late-afternoon sun. A futuristic nightmare supposed to represent the liberation of the spirit of Latin America as seen by a drug-crazed despotic billionaire at the turn of the millennium, to Donovan it resembled the 1939 World's Fair wedded to the Sydney Opera House. A 300-foot-tall silver spire shared space with a 100-foot-tall golden dome and a gold-and-silver palace that looked like a pile of concentric clamshells.

"Damn. It's still there," Donovan swore.

"We must remember to build bigger nukes for the fourth one," Charlie added.

"Is anything on the air?"

"Not a peep. If anyone's home, no one's talking. Most importantly, no targeting radar has been turned on us. Nothing at all is going on."

"Lookouts report no visual sightings on the docks," Percy added.

"Where *are* the docks?" Donovan asked.

"To the left of the dome, which reports say was used as a cocaine storage point," Percy replied.

"Report on the docks."

"No apparent activity," Charlie said. "There's one tanker tied up at the main dock. It was unprotected during the war and may not be in the best of shape."

"Is the city undamaged?"

"Hard to tell at this distance. We'll know when we get closer."

As *Liberator* drew within two miles of shore, the fog lifted and details became apparent. The docks and all waterfront areas visible from the ship were devoid of people. There was no activity anywhere, and of course there were no lights.

"I get structural damage on the north side of the spire," Percy said, peering through binoculars. "There's blast damage and scarring, and a fourth of the external plates are blown off. The direction indicates damage from a blast in the general vicinity of Gatun."

"That's what I think too," Donovan said. "I see damage to the north sides of the sphere and the palace, and surface plates are blown away to the south. The Atlantic-side detonation was over Gatun, and we can see evidence of it in the blast damage to Ciudad Romanus."

Charlie said, "Sensors indicate that radiation has nearly returned to normal background levels. That tanker reads especially hot, though. Steel retains more of the radiation from third-generation nuclear warheads."

"Can we go ashore and for how long?" Donovan asked.

"We can stand outside for an hour. The inside of the city is supposed to be radiation-shielded, so we'll see."

"We *are* just ten miles from a primary target," Percy said. "Do we have to go ashore?"

"There's a coast road that runs parallel to the old canal," Donovan said. "We can use it to take a look at that dam blocking our way to the Atlantic. Chief Smith can get a car going and we'll drive down and have a look."

The sun tempted the horizon and then slipped behind it as *Liberator* cruised the channel in front of Ciudad Romanus. Three miles to the northwest, on the far side of the canal, bonfires sprouted up and dotted the shore like fireflies.

"Fires on the north bank of the Panama Canal, Captain," Percy announced.

"The Panama Canal is history. This is the Panama Strait. As for those fires, they look uncomfortably familiar."

"White-shirts?" Percy asked.

"Not this far south," Charlie said.

"Alex ran a program that modeled white-shirt migration in the Americas," Donovan said. "They could have reached Panama by now."

"And the only thing that's holding them back is this raging water," Charlie said.

"Yeah. If the old canal was still here, they would be tramping through Venezuela by now."

"What if some did get across the strait?"

"I don't see how, but just in case, let's anchor offshore and spend the night watching. We don't know who or what is lurking in those hideous buildings," Donovan said, pointing at Ciudad Romanus.

"Ciudad Romanus is powered by a micronuke," Chief Smith said, peering at the library display that showed the CIA's best information about the layout of the city.

"The first operational one, I hear," Donovan said.

"Yeah. The MicroScale Home Nuclear Unit was developed in France as a European Community export product and test-marketed in Latin America and Southeast Asia."

"I remember now. They tried to crack the Arab market but the Israelis kept blowing them up."

"The Romanus unit was the first sold," Smith went on. "It's supposed to have been installed at the base of the spire and used for two purposes—to power the city's systems and to operate the communications system installed in the upper stories of the spire."

Charlie added, "A communications web that kept track of the positions of all Romanus's coke ships throughout the world. At its best, it kept better track of the drug ships than Lloyds of London kept of Western commerce."

"We can use it, maybe," Donovan said. "If it's still working or can be fixed up, we can listen in to the world—get a fix on colonies of survivors throughout the globe. This radio has got to be more powerful than *Liberator*'s."

"Okay, that gives us another reason to be here," Smith said. "Communications we need—especially a radio that won't betray the ship's position."

Donovan agreed. "Yeah. Every time we broadcast from *Liberator*, I worry that *Nemesis* or some other guy with a bad attitude and a shipful of torpedoes is listening."

"And if there are cars or Jeeps in that city, I can get them going. We had no trouble in other places."

"Do we know anything else about the city?"

"No one is supposed to live in it, at least not in the sphere, which is Romanus's castle. He lived there with whoever he was entertaining at the time."

"Which could include both boys and girls, from what I hear," Donovan said.

"And occasional goats," Charlie added.

"There's a motor pool behind it," Smith concluded. "That's all I know."

"What are the chances of disassembling that micronuke and hauling it back to Espiritu?" Donovan asked.

"On *Liberator*?" Smith asked.

"No. We're going to drag it like an anchor."

"Well, it *was* designed for export by plane, so it must break down into small chunks. If we can get the fuel apart from the core safely, there's no reason we can't take the damn thing home with us. The technical problems would give the engineers on this crew something to labor over."

"And a micronuke could supply all the colonists' power needs indefinitely," Donovan said.

"Yeah. The original idea was to supply cheap power to remote villages as well as to private villas."

"First thing in the morning you get on it," Donovan said.

"And now?" Charlie asked.

"You and me are going hunting."

"For survivors?"

"So to speak. Dr. Fisher needs a warm white-shirt corpse to autopsy, and there figure to be a lot of 'em by those bonfires on the north bank."

Dr. Fisher had taken it upon himself to find a cure for radiation psychosis, the strange postapocalyptic malady that ranged in seriousness from severe delusion to crippling psychosis. White-shirts were examples of the latter. The best examples of the former were two teenagers rescued from the hands of Barbarosa, the maniac who'd tried to take over San Francisco in the wake of World War Three. They had been taken onto *Liberator* and transferred in Tahiti to *Mayflower II* for transport to Espiritu.

To save them as well as the many others like them Dr. Fisher expected to find in their travels, he needed blood and tissue samples. There was no hope of taking a white-shirt alive and the zombielike corpses always deteriorated immediately upon being severely injured. Since white-shirts readily became corpses, all that remained for Donovan and his younger brother to do was pick them up before their comrades could stack them like wood and torch them. This practice resulted in bonfires all along coastal areas infested with white-shirts.

Liberator was anchored a respectful quarter mile offshore of Cuidad Romanus, with armed lookouts posted fore, aft, and on the topside bridge with orders to repel intruders coming from any direction. All the ship's sensors were on automatic, with radar set on short scanning frequencies that could distinguish between a sea gull and a tern. The tidal current was only four knots in that anchorage, but in the deeper channel to the north reached seven knots. That was thought to be enough to prevent white-shirts from crossing the water and getting onto the south shore.

It was not enough to stop one of the ship's inflatables, and shortly after midnight Donovan and Charlie shoved off into the flowing water. Like all excursions away from the ship at night, it was eerie. There were no lights onshore other than the bonfires. Donovan had come to believe that no one who had never experienced total darkness could know the feeling of isolation that derives from seeing no light and knowing there can never be light.

The city behind them was totally dark. Not so much

as a match was glowing. In the absence of artificial light other than the mooring lights on *Liberator* the grotesque skyline of the city was backlit by starlight of the equatorial latitude.

With Charlie in his usual spot in the bow, cradling a Franchi automatic rifle, Donovan opened up the throttle on the inflatable and roared across the canal. As the north bank neared, the bonfires grew larger, and what were bright spots on the shore grew into tall spires of flickering light, with illuminated smoke curling into the sky. The fires sparkled off the canal water and lit the way to shore.

Under half a mile away, Donovan cut speed to one-quarter and proceeded slowly. The bonfires were spaced every half mile along the north bank from one horizon to the other.

"How many fires do they need?" Donovan said.

"There were a lot of bodies left over by the war," Charlie said. "Slow down more... I'm picking up floaters."

"Logs or bodies?"

"Bodies. Logs burn quicker."

Donovan saw what his brother was talking about—white-shirt bodies bobbed in the water just like logs coming down the stream from a lumbering camp. In the darkness they were lit only by the inflatable's bow light and reflection from a nearby bonfire, but Donovan guessed there was one every hundred feet, rolling and bobbing as the current swept it along towards the Atlantic.

"Where do all these guys come from?" he wondered out loud, slowing the raft even more and turning her bow into the current to run along the north bank.

They approached a bonfire, flaring madly just twenty feet from the bank. The swift current had been tearing through the isthmus for three months and had already worn away the north bank to the point where the original land was only a memory. Donovan thought he saw the remains of a street and a row of homes that had been first flattened and then torn up. The fire was built of available materials. The white-shirts, in addition to burning bodies, burned loose wood.

Bits of wood paneling from houses and studs from their frames went onto the fire, which was tended by eight or ten men.

"I never saw them up close before," Donovan said.

"Other than the one whose face you flattened," Charlie added.

In the battle for San Francisco, Donovan put his fist—literally—into the face of a white-shirt who tried to kill him. The radiation damage was such that the man's skull bones collapsed like an overripe melon, a sight that filled Donovan with sufficient disgust to order a tactical nuclear strike on the white-shirts' HQ.

For a fleeting moment he had thought that he had ended the white-shirts' reign of terror. He was wrong.

The white-shirts tending the fire carried wood scavenged from the ruined buildings on the north side of the canal. As the flames grew, they consumed a steady stream of bodies dragged out of the rubble by other white-shirts. Twin trails of them snaked out of the ruins, carrying bodies large and small for cremation.

"I've seen some weird shit in my travels, but this one escapes me," Donovan said.

"Amen to that. It's one of the odder compulsions I've noted, too."

"At least it helps clean up the mess. These guys are cheaper than robots and neater than vultures. It only pisses me off when they start making bodies of their own to burn. The survivors have been through enough shit without this."

"Look down here," Charlie said, pointing upstream.

There, a sparse trail of white-shirts stood at the edge of the water, the man nearest the edge stretching his arms toward the south bank, where no white-shirt had yet reached.

After under a minute of reaching out for the far shore, as if magically preparing his way across the raging water, the white-shirt suddenly lurched forward into the water. As Donovan and Charlie watched, he flapped his arms for a few seconds and then was dragged under by the current. Soon he joined the legion of drowned bodies bobbing in the stream.

"Lemmings," Donovan said.

"Yeah. Let's hear it for the moat."

"This torrent is keeping the loonies on the north bank, out of South America. Maybe the survivors there have a better chance."

"Computer projections for World War Three always held that the Southern Hemisphere would suffer the least damage," Charlie said.

"Did you see that guy reaching out? I wonder what he was looking at."

Donovan turned back toward Ciudad Romanus and saw it right away. Near the top of the spire a light glowed, looking a bit like the eye atop the pyramid on the great seal of the United States. Donovan had kept a few dollar bills as souvenirs of the way things used to be, and swore to look at one when he got back to the ship.

"There's a light on in the spire," Charlie said, staring at it, too.

"Somebody's home after all," Donovan said.

Alex selected for her home and office one of the larger huts, one between a blaze of hibiscus and the stone *marae*. The altar still made her nervous, but she reasoned it would be better to be close to that particular source of power. If for no other reason than that the natives, should they return, would respect it.

The colonists' first night was a frenzied one. The task of getting fifty or sixty weary travelers, who had come halfway around the world on a wooden boat ashore on a tropical island with no dock, proved to be a harrowing one.

The tide was out when they arrived and the coral nearly exposed. Four hours later, when the fleet could get over the reef, the anchors dragged in the soft sand. More-or-less permanent moorings were driven into the coral, and the fleet was anchored safely, with *Mayflower II* on the outside providing shelter from the waves.

Getting them ashore was a task akin to landing an unprepared army on a hostile beach. They came ashore in dinghies or if too impatient, swam. By the time all were up at the settlement eight hours had passed and a full tropical moon shone on the stone altar. By midnight all had chosen huts and most had fallen into exhausted sleep.

They had space to live and sleep in for the first time in months, and in the first bursts of enthusiasm selected shelters that were spread all over the plateau. As the early morning hours approached and jungle sounds swept down over them for the first time, Jennings and Alex first pondered the wisdom of such dispersal.

Jennings sat on one of the woven-palm mats that served as beds and shook his head over an attempt to chart the colonists' new homes on paper.

"This is a nightmare," he said at last. "Half of them could wander off and get lost and it would be daybreak before we knew it."

"I should have thought of this before," Alex admitted. "Planning a community isn't so easy when everyone arrives on-site at once."

"We don't even have lights for them all. There are three communal fires out there . . . no more."

"I don't know how bad that is. There are no dangerous animals on these islands. Mainly sand crabs, and they don't bite badly enough to worry about."

"Rats imported by passing ships are my worry."

"I haven't seen any," Alex said. "This place is too off the beaten track to get many ships. There simply are no predators here—man is on top of the food chain."

"What a frightening prospect," Jennings said.

At that moment, there came from off in the jungle a far-off wail. Jennings swore it came from a timber wolf, and dropped the paper he was scribbling on.

"On second thought . . ."

"What was that?" Alex asked.

"It sounded like a wolf. I know that's impossible."

"It's more than impossible. It's crazy."

The wail sounded again, reverberating through the thick jungle foliage like a stab in the night.

"I wonder if man is still on top of the food chain," Jennings said, looking around nervously.

The waterfront of Ciudad Romanus was sleek and barren. Designed to replicate the promenade along New York's East River near the United Nations, where the young Romanus had his first political experience as military attaché to the UN legation, it was meant for strollers and joggers on Sunday afternoons. The problem was that most Panamanians were too poor for recreational exercise and not let into Romanus anyway. And the residents of that imperial city, mainly the general and his staff, were disinclined to do anything more strenuous than sleep on Sunday afternoons.

The appearance of a light in the upper spire told Donovan that, at the very least, the micronuke still worked. Power was being generated, at least enough to light one bulb. That was more than they saw elsewhere in the western world, and it implied human intention. The odds of such a strategically placed bulb being lit by chance were infinitesimal.

Donovan and Charlie returned to *Liberator* long enough to outfit a second inflatable with officers and crew and acquire two armed guards of their own. Ship's sensors still registered nothing from the city, but it was clear to Donovan that someone had gotten the micronuke working and was puttering around in the transmitter room. That was what he would do in the same situation—get the juice turned on and call for help.

The Romanus promenade had no provision for tying up a boat. That was unsurprising, especially in light of the several machine gun emplacements with muzzles facing across the canal. No one was *supposed* to tie up there, and those foolish enough to try were supposed to be strafed. But no one remained to man them, and Charlie tossed a line around a stanchion and hauled himself up onto the promenade.

Before Donovan could even get onshore, Charlie inspected a machine gun mount and said, "This is a brand-new Walther PB AutoStrafe, and there are four more like it."

Donovan yelled, "Chief!"

"Yo, boss," Chief Smith answered, the last of the landing party to huff and puff his way to shore.

"We can use some machine guns on board. We are

no longer strictly a submersible. There could be surface action, and we now have women and children to protect."

"I'll have them removed and put on board," Smith replied, taking out his transceiver and calling the ship.

The promenade was ten yards wide and decorated with stone benches placed every fifty feet. It looked like a movie set on an off day, pretty but very artificial.

Donovan looked up at the three buildings that dominated the sky from that point of view. Of the three, looking like a sphere, a spire, and a clam, the spire was nearest.

It had doors that from a distance appeared to be glass, but turned out to be made of a tougher material. Smith said, "I don't believe it—this place has been using Shield Glass."

The dark-tinted, laser-reaction "glass" was made of clear fiber plastic and composites, capable of withstanding a direct hit from a 20-mm shell. Shield Glass was used in vital parts in *Liberator*—the topside bridge viewports, the two laser turrets—and also served as the matrix for the Cyclops display. Shield Glass was also a selective conductor of light waves, which allowed activation of the Cyclops LCD display.

"This glass has got to be wired for a security system," Smith said, tapping it with the butt of his gun.

"Set it off," Donovan said. "Who's inside to call the cops? What cops would they call?"

"I'll find out," Percy said, waving the four armed guards to join him.

"Good idea. Take a patrol around the back of this building. Check for other exits, and generally see if anyone's around. Call if there's a problem."

"Yes, sir." The hurriedly assembled patrol began to circle the base of the spire, which occupied roughly a city block.

A torch was sent ashore from the ship, and soon a machinist's mate was burning away the lock plate. As the glass melted away, Smith could see the telltale flashes of an optical security system being set off.

"It's a silent alarm and it's gone off," he reported.

"We'll soon find out how dead everyone is," Donovan said, fingering his Colt.

"I don't think there's anyone around," Charlie noted. "I got the same feeling I got in Papeete—the joint's deserted."

"Papeete wasn't blastproof."

"Yeah, but this war proved to be a lot weirder than everyone predicted. Whole populations have disappeared without a clue. Timber wolves are prowling city streets and sharks are multiplying like crazy. Do they have wolves in Central America?"

"No. Mostly there are jaguars."

"What a comforting thought," Charlie said. "Remember to sit with your back to the wall."

The lock fell inward with a clatter that revealed a marble floor.

"Spare no expense," Donovan commented, peering in through the smoldering hole.

The ten-foot door swung open, leading to a wide lobby decorated with benches that, like the floor, were made of dark-grained marble. Neo–social realist paintings from the post–Central American War period were hung on walls made of polished white stone.

Recessed lighting, invisible from the outside due to the Shield Glass, illuminated the lobby. Even the elevator buttons glowed. As the centerpiece of the lobby, a marble fountain decorated with fiber optics that spread out to form a gigantic poppy flower was still spraying water into the still cavern of the building.

"What if you gave a party and no one came?" Donovan asked.

His transceiver crackled, and Percy reported, "Nothing doing out back, Captain. Like everywhere else, it's as dead as you get."

"They must have had troops in this city. Where did they keep them?"

Charlie said, "The CIA thought that Romanus was too paranoid about coups after that business in '97 to keep troops in the citadel."

"Are there barracks outside the citadel?" Donovan asked.

"Not anymore," Percy replied.

"Blown away?"

"Flattened and abandoned. However, the whiteshirts haven't gotten here yet. There are tons of corpses. You ought to come out back and smell it."

"Thanks a lot. What else can you see?"

"The rubble of blown-away buildings for miles. After that, jungle. There is some motion along the forest line, but I can't see what it is. It's at least five miles away."

"Jaguars," Donovan said.

"Permission to come into the citadel," Percy asked.

"Granted. Join me in the lobby."

When Percy and his men rejoined the others, Donovan left guards in the lobby and on the promenade and took the elevator. Chief Smith had determined that there was enough juice to run it. The micronuke was positioned in the back of the spire's base, and purring away as if there had been no war. From it, power cables ran not only into the spire but also to the sphere and the clam, but according to the control panel probably nowhere else.

"Romanus wanted his power, but he didn't want to share it," Smith reported, wiping his greasy hands on a rag.

"The micronuke only feeds the buildings?" Donovan asked.

"Yeah, and I got a handle on how he survived without a staff. There's a lot of automation around here. The climate control, lights, everything. The power also feeds the alarm system, which alerts the guards in the barracks out back."

"Who are now dead."

"Which means that no one will shoot at us, unless it's the guy who turned on the light upstairs. According to

93

the security system's log, no one has been in or out of this building in over three months."

"When the war started."

"Yeah. We'll finally get a handle on exactly when."

Donovan said, "Let's go up and introduce ourselves."

The elevator rose slowly, stopping at each floor and holding there while Percy and two armed guards checked things out.

The first four floors held kitchens and food-storage areas. There was enough food stored there to feed a small army, and most of it was in a highly preserved state. Quick checks with the EnviroTester showed that all the food, as well as the bottled water, was safe. Romanus's blast shielding had done its designed job of keeping out radiation.

Floors five through seven were housing for staff, all of whom had disappeared. Floors eight through ten were offices, vacant and apparently never used. From floor eleven up through the communications room on floor twenty-seven there was nothing. The floors were empty, never designed to do anything useful and never occupied. Increasingly, Donovan was seeing Romanus's citadel city as nothing more than a hollow testament to a monumental ego. It was all show. Perhaps one reason he never let visitors in was that there was nothing inside to show them.

"Whoever's up there will know we're coming," Smith said as a computer-generated voice announced, in Spanish, their arrival on the twenty-seventh floor.

"It's got to be the general himself," Donovan said as the doors swung open.

And it was. General Hector Romanus sat in an immense leather swivel chair, holding a small-caliber automatic aimed at the elevator door.

"Drop it," Charlie ordered, hefting his Franchi.

"Who are you?" Romanus asked, his initial look of terror having changed to one of curiosity. He hadn't seen so many gringos in a long time.

"Drop the gun and we'll tell you," Donovan said.

Romanus shrugged and tossed the gun away. It skittered along the hardwood floor.

"Tom Donovan commanding the U.S.S. *Liberator*."

"The submarine? I have heard of it. Where is it?"

"In the canal, or what remains of the canal."

"I did not see it. How long have you been there?"

"Since late afternoon."

"That explains it. I have been occupied with events to the south."

"What events?" Donovan asked.

"The war."

"The war is over."

"That war I know little about, except that my citadel withstood it. I refer to the coming war with my enemies from the Andes. Who are these men with you, Captain?"

"My officers: Chief Smith, First Officer Percy, Chief Gunnery Officer Donovan, who also is my brother."

"I am Hector Romanus. Welcome to my communications room."

He swept his arm around to show off the interior, which was a dazzling display of up-to-date radio and telecommunications equipment, much of it in a curving oak console that resembled the bridge of a starship. Two huge speakers mounted at the junction of the wall and the ceiling crackled with static. Beyond the console was another room lined with windows. That high up in the spire, the floor space was quite small and Romanus had built an observation room adjacent to the radio equipment.

The general himself was just as Donovan remembered him from pictures: quite small, wearing a slept-in uniform replete with medals, with graying black hair combed to cover a bald spot, and cheeks that still showed the signs of childhood acne scars.

"Very impressive," Donovan said. "Have you been able to reach anyone?"

"Not as yet. However, there are men out there. I have heard chatter in English, Spanish and Russian. Most of it I could not understand. However, I am no linguist. Neither am I a communications specialist."

"My brother is the latter. May he?"

"Of course," Romanus said, moving his chair to one side so that Charlie could get to the main operator's station. "Now I ask you," he said to Donovan. "Why are you here?"

"Why? We were trying to get to the Atlantic, of course."

"What on earth for?"

"Our mission is to rescue survivors. There are some in New York."

"What a quaint notion... the submarine captain attempts to pick up the pieces after the world has ended. Do you expect to succeed?"

"I expect to die trying, which is more than you appear to be doing. What *are* you doing, by the way?"

"Trying to communicate with my men. What do you think?"

"We did not see any men," Donovan said, looking at Percy.

"They are in the southern jungle, fighting my enemies."

"What enemies? I mean, what enemies other than all of mankind?"

"Patino and Gital, from Colombia. Surely you have heard of them."

"They're the two cocaine barons who survived the Central American War and negotiated the Licensed Narcotics Control Act with the UN."

That treaty, which ended the open fighting in Central America in 1996, made cocaine a legal but controlled substance in the same category as tobacco and grain alcohol. Its passage was a bitter pill for American politicians to swallow, but necessary to stop the loss of life on both sides in Central America and, not insignificantly, to produce revenues for the U.S. government. Under its terms, each nation's government was in charge of street-level distribution and kept those profits. In the first year of operation, the Licensed Narcotics Control Act produced sufficient revenue to fund the complete revamping of the American education system. In its second, controlled cocaine paid for a national health plan.

"Why are they fighting you now?" Donovan asked.

"They are after my money. The same thing as always."

"What good will money do them now?"

"It's in the form of gold, in my vault in the Great Hall of the People."

"The Great Hall? Oh, the clam. I noted the design. But gold is now useful only for making fishing sinkers. Haven't you gotten the idea—we've had World War Three, for God's sake. No one's sitting around counting cash."

"That will change," Romanus said.

"It will change in a hundred years if there are enough survivors to go around. But you and I won't see it, and our children, if we are lucky enough to have any, will be in a small-village fishing economy for generations. The world as we knew it is dead. Which brings me to a key point—who pulled the trigger?"

"And started World War Three? Why do you care?"

"There has been some betting. I have a few bucks in the pool myself," Donovan said sarcastically.

"It was the Germans, who else? They did it as the first official act of the Fourth Reich."

Donovan was astounded. "The Fourth Reich?"

"They didn't call it that. Give the bastards credit for *some* taste. But start it they did."

"But Germany only achieved complete freedom from Four Power supervision in March," Percy protested.

"And in May they were on the march," Romanus said. "This was on the TV. Where were you guys?"

"Under the Arctic ice on maneuvers," Donovan said.

"When we surfaced it was over."

"You missed quite a show. My two port cities were completely blown away. Fortunately, my citadel withstood the blast. Not so lucky, my canal. It is blocked at the Atlantic side. I imagine you noticed that."

"It did come to our attention."

"I have not ventured out to see it, but my men tell me of a gigantic earthen dam—an immense waterfall, if you will. It can be seen from the south window. Go have a look, though it is dark out."

"We have night vision binoculars," Percy said.

"I will buy them. How much do you want?"

"Not for sale. Percy, go see."

"Yes, sir," he replied, and went off into the observation room with two of his men.

"I can't raise New York on the radio," Charlie said. "That frequency is still dead. However, there is something on a channel typically used by the British. Let me try to pull it in."

"You will find nothing of consequence," Romanus said. "All technology is still down other than in my citadel."

"I don't suppose you videotaped the war," Donovan said.

"Of course not. What do I look like, a recording engineer? I am fighting my own war."

"Do you *remember* how the Germans started the big one?"

"Details are fragmentary and memory fades," Romanus said, getting irritated by the questioning. "There was some saber rattling over the boundary with Poland."

"Nothing ever changes," Donovan sighed.

"There was a lot of argument over what the Germans saw as trade restrictions imposed by Russia. There was argument over German minorities in Czechoslovakia. The word *lebensraum* was tossed around. And there was some flap over a submarine."

"A what?"

"A submarine. Your sort of thing."

The specter of *Nemesis* instantly hung over the proceedings, as Donovan recalled Charlie's having seen her threaten the Sea of Japan conference and fire a missile.

"Describe it."

"I don't know what it looks like. It was an advanced secret project, the submersible equivalent of the *Bismarck*. Something the Germans were working on before reunification but without telling anyone. There was some arguing over the submarine between Berlin, Moscow, and Washington, and then one morning, poof!"

Donovan thought: Jesus, they did it again. They started their third world war in 100 years and this time succeeded in blowing away the planet. Not only that, but the submarine behind it all was still out there, trying to kill *Liberator*.

"Did the motherfuckers *survive* their latest venture?" Donovan asked.

"Unknown. Suddenly the lights went out. Except in here, of course."

"And you have heard nothing from the world."

"Periodic static . . . an occasional voice. No more. I can't be bothered to listen."

"Charlie?" Donovan asked.

"Nothing yet. I'll keep working on it."

Percy reported back from the other room: "That dam is real enough, but not as big as we thought. It's only a few hundred yards thick—the southern end of a huge bomb crater. We may be able to break through with a torpedo."

"Anything bigger than a pinprick will cause the water pressure to cave it in," Smith said.

"Then we can do it."

"I'll have to compute the effect of a torpedo hit on an earthen structure," Percy said. "It's possible that the earth will absorb the force of the blow."

"That about a Mark 97N missile?" Donovan asked.

"That will do it, no doubt," Percy said. "And since that land has already been nuked once . . ."

"And is deserted."

"I have no moral dilemma with nuking it again."

"You guys have nuclear weapons?" Romanus exclaimed, perking up. All of a sudden, a solution to his war with his neighbors presented itself.

"Wipe that eager look off your face. There are only a handful left and I plan to use them well."

"I was merely seeking a solution to my problem."

"What problem? Oh, your 'war.' Tell me about it."

"Patino and Gital, from Colombia. From the end of the Central American War until three months ago, they fought each other. Now they fight me. They want the gold from the vault as well as a large shipment that remains in a tanker in the harbor."

"You said 'fight.' With what army are you fighting?"

"Fifty men only. They were inside the citadel with me when the bombs fell, and survived, along with a dozen of my personal staff, who are now on a guarded trip to the inner city to look for survivors from their own families."

"Patino and Gital—what armies do they have?" Donovan asked.

"They claim a thousand men and many arms. But I have information that it is two hundred men and small arms. My fifty will destroy their two hundred."

"I personally have no interest in this matter," Donovan said. "You are fighting over nothing. Over less than nothing. The best that you all can do is band together for survival and get the hell out of this region of earth, which is highly radioactive."

"My citadel is safe," Romanus insisted.

"Until the food and water run out, which should be any day. You've supported between fifty and seventy-five people for three months on supplies. It can't last. You have no choice but to make peace and head for the hills. It should be relatively safe in the Andes."

"But my enemies are in the Andes," the general protested.

"Like I said, make peace. I'll be glad to negotiate it."

"Out of the question."

There was a commotion in the observation room.

The man that Percy had left in there watching the approaches to the city rushed in, yelling "Men moving this way from the jungle! Other men in pursuit!"

"Put the ship on alert!" Donovan snapped.

15

The force coming out of the jungle was entirely on foot, and if it were possible to raise a cloud of dust in a swamp, that's what they were doing.

Three columns of men fled on foot from an approaching enemy whose presence could be deduced by tracers, rocket fire, and mortar detonations.

"My men," Romanus exclaimed, having run to the observation room to watch with the others.

"Did you say that Patino and Gital have only small arms?" Donovan asked.

"Those were the reports."

"Shoot the messenger," Donovan advised, watching as Romanus's "army" of fifty men walked, stumbled, and ran through the swamps that stood between Ciudad Romanus and the southern jungle.

"They will be safe once they're behind the walls," the dictator proclaimed.

"This place is protected from a flank attack by a security fence that mixes lasers with old-fashioned barbed wire," Smith said. "It will keep infantry out for a while, but won't hold. The fence is anchored at posts that can be blown away with select fire."

"Are you sure you're a general?" Donovan asked.

"I will crush my enemies," Romanus insisted. "And you too if you won't join me."

"I have other things to do, and won't get involved in this bullshit so long as you stay out of my hair."

"I must go to see my men," Romanus announced.

103

"Go," Donovan said. "But remember, I can turn your citadel into taco sauce in ten seconds. Don't irritate me."

Romanus gave a stiff salute, then rode the elevator down. Donovan watched him go, then returned his attention to the ragtag group of men who were now within a mile of relative safety, while their pursuers were beginning to emerge from the jungle.

"What a motley crew. At least they're not white-shirts."

"No, but *they're* right on the other side of the canal," Percy said.

"And we're in the middle," Smith added.

"Have the Walther PB AutoStrafes removed from their installations and taken back to the ship right away," Donovan ordered.

"Romanus has a command center in the clam," Percy said. "My men found it a few minutes ago."

"He'll be taking reports from his field commanders there," Donovan said.

"Should I start taking apart the micronuke?" Smith asked.

"No. They need it, at least for a few more days. Once they realize how implausible their position is and acknowledge the need to make peace and blow town we'll steal the power plant. For the time being, let's make sure we're safe from these banana republic warriors."

Alex didn't have much weapons training, being at heart a Ph.D. from San Francisco with an interest in environmental engineering, but that didn't prevent her from hefting her Franchi like a pro.

With Jennings she walked the perimeter of the settlement, a task complicated by the fact that many of the huts were built right up against the forest line.

Even at three in the morning the fires blazed on, tended by volunteers who were among the very few too sleepy to bed down the second they arrived. After months at sea, the chance to build a big fire and sit around it was irresistible.

Both of them heard the howls, and both believed there were wolves in the jungle. The fact that it was impossible—or at the very least made no sense—did not carry much weight on their first night in that strange and faraway place. They were frightened and wanted explanations that made sense.

Alex and Jennings had none. The presence of wolves in San Francisco was a strange phenomenon, but could at least be explained. Unhindered by man or competition, and starved for food, they walked out of the Sierra Nevadas and up the peninsula into the city. But wolves in the South Pacific?

"No way," Alex said.

"There's no other explanation. The top of this island's food chain is—or was—man. Apart from nasty monkeys, the animals don't get big or fierce. That's one of the reasons they call this Paradise."

"Paradise with timber wolves *and* a volcano," Alex said, thinking at that instant that Donovan would find it ironic. She missed him, and wondered how he was doing on his expedition into the Atlantic.

At the western boundary of the settlement, a broad trail led away from civilization and to the foot of the volcano. It was amazingly nearby; maybe a mile or more, considering the towering height of the cone that seemed almost on top of them.

From the darkness of the nighttime jungle, parrots squawked and monkeys whistled. Then, every few minutes, would come one of the howls. One howl was from the north side of the volcano, another two from the south. The sounds met and echoed in the dense foliage, sometimes drawing nearer, then at last settling in about a half mile away.

That half mile could have been a light-year, the jungle was that thick and the night that dark. Alex sat on a tree stump and Jennings sat on the soft jungle turf at her feet. Both held their automatics aimed down the path, occasionally sweeping their lines of sight through the black jungle. After half an hour, the howls got no closer, although every time a howl came the parrots and monkeys shut up in fear.

"We're not imagining this," Alex said. "The monkeys don't like it either."

"Lie down and to go to sleep for a few hours," Jennings said. "I'll take the first watch."

"Paradise isn't supposed to be like this," she told him.

"You had no right to steal my guns!" Romanus thundered, pounding a too-long-pampered fist into a soft palm.

"They were aimed at my ship," Donovan replied. "That makes me uneasy."

"I could have used them against my enemies. I *need* them."

"To fight the enemy that has only small arms? I think not. Besides, we counted six good machine gun emplacements facing the swamp and jungle. They will do you. Combined with this fortress, you should do better than hold your own against a superior force."

"You have no right to play God!" Romanus yelled.

"Someone has to. The old God seriously fucked up the world. I can't do any worse."

Smith said, "See the reason, General. Make peace. I estimate that you have enough food and water to supply your men for another three days. After that you're dead."

"We're leaving whether you live or die," Donovan went on. "If we can't make it into the Atlantic, we'll go back to the Pacific. And you can't stay here—it's too hot; the ground, the air, the water. You can't stay inside the citadel more than three days and you'll fry outside. There are white-shirts to the north, and we've explained what they'll do to you given half the chance. Your only hope is to make peace with Patino and Gital and move to the relative safety of the Andes and other isolated areas of the South American mainland."

"I'm not picking up radio from there, but the computer indicates it should have escaped the worst of the war," Charlie said.

"Patino and Gital want my gold," Romanus insisted.

"Give it to them." Donovan shrugged. "It's not worth anything."

"I worked hard for my fortune."

"I won't debate the point," Donovan said.

"How about a trade?" suggested a new voice, one Donovan had only just been introduced to. He was Mendosa, Romanus's field commander, a lieutenant colonel in the Panamanian army and the only man among Romanus's legion with combat experience.

A younger man of fifty with the hardened look of someone who had labored too long in the sun at unsavory business, Mendosa had an attitude of deceit that turned Donovan off. He was hungry, even more so than a desperate man would be expected to be. And sticking around to help Romanus clean up his mess hardly seemed the avocation of this gentleman.

"You ain't got nothin' we want," said Charlie, who liked Mendosa a good deal less than his brother.

"I realize that gold doesn't interest you. It would not even make good bullets. But we can give you something better—a way into the Atlantic and a solid fighting force."

"We have both," Donovan said. "We can blast our way through that dam—at least I'm pretty sure we can—and my men have shown themselves to be pretty good in a fight."

Mendosa laughed. "Your men are engineers and Ph.D.s, not soldiers."

"Don't underestimate them. A Russian sub crew did that and died."

"My men are experienced jungle fighters, and all the world is a jungle now."

"They're great at running out of jungles," Donovan said. "I watched them half an hour ago."

"They withdrew to solid defensive positions," Mendosa argued.

The argument was ended when a brace of mortar

rounds landed close enough to the Great Hall of the People to rattle the blast shielding and give an already shaky Romanus a bad case of the nerves.

"The Huns are at the gates of the city," Donovan said.

"My defensive perimeter will hold them," Romanus said.

"I want to go out and watch this," Donovan said, and led the way there.

The back of the Great Hall looked less like a stack of clamshells than the front, Romanus having spent money mainly on the design of the facade. The south border was functional, appropriate to the side facing a swamp and a jungle.

The six machine gun emplacements protected the landlocked sides of the citadel. They were positioned atop a ten-foot concrete wall that reminded Donovan of pictures he had seen of the old Berlin Wall. Romanus's wall went completely around the citadel, a distance of about ten blocks. Beneath it was a fifty-foot-wide trench, dug within the past few years, that also served as a dirt road for trucks and Jeeps. The road ran south to what remained of Panama City and the other cities of the southern coast, and north to what remained of Gatun and the Atlantic coastal cities. Between the citadel and the swamp there lay the ruined living quarters where Romanus's staff lived. It was blown down and partly burned, and the only things that moved in it were vultures feeding off the still-rotting corpses.

It was nearly four in the morning with dawn a good two hours off. The sky had not yet begun to lighten, and only night vision equipment allowed Donovan to see what was going on outside the citadel. The forces of Patino and Gital, after chasing Romanus's men out of the jungle and across the swamp, had stopped their advance and were holding positions on the jungle's edge. Their campfires glowed brazenly.

"Those guys never heard the expression 'three on a match,' " Donovan said.

"Clearly they're unafraid of Romanus," Percy said.

Romanus's men were bivouacked along the wall, where tents and lean-tos were set up. They were not allowed in the city—Romanus was too afraid of coups to allow more than a few men near him—but had to camp in the dirt between the wall and the remains of the outside city. A small effort had been made to clean up bodies in the months since the war, and no corpses were within sight or—unless the wind blew from the south—smell of the wall.

Donovan looked down at them and felt something like pity. "This is like the Christians and the lions," he said.

"Yeah," Charlie agreed. "With Caesar up in the grandstand giving the thumbs-down."

"Have you stopped feeling bad about our stealing his guns and power plant?"

"It was only a passing weakness. Percy is having six more men come ashore to bolster our weapons party."

"Very good. Did the ship detect anything?"

"No threats. However, there were some radio transmissions locally."

"Radio? What kind?"

"Hand-held transceivers. Patino was directing his troops."

"What kind of range do they have?"

"They can listen up to four miles . . . transmit over a mile of open land."

"Can we tap in and talk to them?"

"Already arranged," Charlie said proudly, handing his big brother a modified transceiver.

"What talk did you pick up?" Donovan asked.

"Orders . . . some strategy. Patino is running the show. No mention of Gital. They're bedded down for the night at the edge of the swamp, waiting for daylight. I guess they mean to attack at dawn. Maybe they want to see the defenses of the citadel."

Donovan fingered the transmit button, then mused, "I wish I spoke Spanish."

"Patino has been around the world. Try English."

Donovan spoke into the transceiver: "This is Tom Donovan, commanding the U.S.S. *Liberator* now moored in the Panama Canal. Patino, are you there? I hope so, cause I can save us all a lot of trouble."

16

The transport doors at the southeast corner of the citadel were made of early blast-resistant carbon-fiber neosteel, which was light but on the thick side. Neosteel that was produced before the turn of the millennium tended to run up to four inches thick in its blast-resistant configuration, and thus was suitable mainly for building material where thickness didn't matter. Post-2000 neosteel was stronger and thinner, and found uses in the keel and ribs of *Liberator*.

The doors were forty feet high and set at the base of a ramp that led from ground level outside down to the subbasement of the citadel. They swung open, powered by hydraulics. "One more thing that won't work when the power goes off," Chief Smith noted. Lately he had been de-technologizing himself in preparation for making a home on Espiritu; paring down to an absolute minimum the number of technology-dependent systems.

Once open, the doors yawned wide to admit the first rays of a new dawn. Outside, a paved road went a half mile to the east, where it narrowed and then followed the southern bank of the canal toward Gatun. Three Jeeps stood on the tarmac, having just been rescued from the wreckage of the motor pool and whipped into running condition.

"None of these pieces of junk are going to run at Indianapolis this year, but they'll get us to Gatun and back."

"I don't imagine the road is in too good shape within a mile or two of the crater," Donovan said, hoping he was wrong.

"It could be passable. That crater looks pretty deep, meaning that the blast was nearly ground-level and a lot of the force went up. Ground-hugging structures outside of the immediate blast area could be okay."

"Meaning?"

"Meaning roads and occasional lean-tos," Smith said.

"Which doesn't mean that you should stay outside all day," Dr. Fisher said, waving the probe of his Enviro-Tester around the dank dawn air outside the compound.

"How's the environmental index today, Doctor?" Donovan asked.

"In a word, it sucks."

"How long can we stay outside the citadel?"

"Three hours max. One hour would be better. And I want to check your tags the second you get back."

All shore personnel wore radiation identity tags that displayed, on a digital display, how much radiation they had been exposed to. The tags were designed for engine room workers and others who had regular contact with *Liberator*'s nuclear power plant, but also served for outside work in contaminated areas.

Dr. Fisher came ashore on the crest of his obsession with finding a cure for radiation psychosis. He still needed bodies to autopsy, and there were plenty of them in Panama. Both behind the citadel and across the river, among the white-shirts. Crewmen had ventured across the canal in inflatables and brought back samples, and had added to them partially decomposed bodies from the living space behind the citadel.

Romanus objected mightily to having his subbasement turned into a temporary morgue, but preferred the basement to the lobby of the spire, for that was the choice Donovan gave him.

Gleaming stainless steel food-preparation tables were converted for autopsy use, and the compound's medical quarters was stripped of masks, sample bottles, and other equipment. With jury-rigged lighting provided by the engineering crew, Dr. Fisher hacked happily at the bodies, removing tissue and organ samples and carefully preserving them in indexed bottles. He would use the ship's advanced CD Rom diagnostics to find out how the men died.

Donovan got into the lead Jeep alongside Chief Smith, who drove. Charlie half stood, half sat in back, as always sweeping the horizon with his Franchi. The two other Jeeps were filled with crewmen and ammo. First Officer Percy was back on board *Liberator* with one finger on the trigger, as had become standard practice when Donovan was making visit on alien shores. One word from the captain, and Percy would launch a torpedo or a nuclear-tipped missile, or both, depending on the situation. This practice had made Donovan's life easier in several situations.

As the convoy started up, Donovan asked, "Where are we meeting Patino?"

"At the town three miles down the road," Charlie said. "There's a gas station next to a truck stop."

"Are they open for breakfast? I haven't been waited on for months."

"You mean Alex doesn't make breakfast?"

"I make breakfast," Donovan said. "Something I learned from Dad."

"How many cans of Dinty Moore Beef Stew can one family eat?" Charlie mused.

"That was before Mom and him got married. After they got together he threw out the can opener. He got to make a pretty mean bean sprout omelet. You would know this if you hadn't slept until noon every day of your young life."

"I was resting," Charlie said, with an early-morning yawn.

"For what? And how do we know this gas station and truck stop are still there?"

"Patino told me. His men have been all over this countryside, at least that part of it south of the canal. It's the citadel they can't get into."

Donovan said, "Does Patino know that he's fighting for control of nothing?"

"Sure. I mean, I guess he knows that gold has been rendered pointless. But listen, Tom . . . we've just had World War III. Not everyone is thinking as straight as you and me. Maybe continuing to fight is one more symptom of radiation insanity. Did you think of that?"

"Dr. Fisher has it down as a possibility."

"Anyway, Patino scouted out this road. He said the buildings we're going to are intact. The town is just to the east of one of the few dry routes out of the swamp."

"I don't trust this guy," Smith said.

"Neither do I, but we have to get past him in order to scout out the dam," Donovan said. "We can't do our work here if we have to worry about him shooting at us."

"Maybe he can postpone attacking the citadel until after we split," Charlie said.

"That's what I'm hoping."

The three-Jeep convoy roared down the increasingly narrow paved road, skirting clumps of uprooted trees and blown-down roadside shacks, until all of the citadel with the exception of the spire was out of sight behind them.

The little town was no more. Only shards of buildings remained, and what there was resembled a house of cards that had been blown down. But here and there a good part of a building stood, including the gas station and attendant diner. Both of them were intact, save for blown-out windows and tons of debris that had been blown over from less-fortunate nearby buildings.

Four men stood by the solitary pump, cradling AK-47s. They were unshaven and wore jungle camouflage, and one of them looked nervously from the approaching Jeeps to a patch of woods across the street. There, six and maybe more men stood, making no attempt to conceal themselves.

The Jeeps pulled up and stopped their engines by the pumps. Donovan jumped out and shook Patino's hand, noting that, with his scruffy beard, he looked like archive photos of Fidel Castro.

"How goes the revolution?" Donovan asked.

"Not bad. Señor Romanus cannot hold us off forever. So, Captain, why are you in Panama? Do you too have a taste for gold?"

"No way. It would only weigh down my ship. I presume you know that gold is useless."

"Of course. Only a madman would want gold for use now. I think of my children. I have many, and they too will have sons. In their lifetimes gold will once again be valuable."

"Maybe," Donovan allowed.

"So, I take the gold for them, and go back to my farm in Colombia. I will live in peace and harmony with nature, the same as I did for years before this ghastly war."

"How much of Colombia is left?" Donovan asked. "How much of *South America* is left?"

"My farm is intact, as are adjacent farms. To the best of my knowledge, most of the people of the Andes have survived. Even the coca fields are intact. I find in that a certain irony."

"Me too. My government tried to kill you off in a limited war ten or fifteen years ago, and that failed. Now we had World War III and destroyed most of the planet, yet the cocaine crop is intact."

"And Patino is still alive. There is a lesson to be learned," Patino said.

"What of Gital?"

"Alive, and advancing with his men on Romanus from the west."

"Is that true?" Donovan asked his brother.

"If they're moving on foot and staying off the airwaves we'd have no way of knowing," Charlie replied.

"Gital has a hundred men . . . okay, maybe he has fifty . . . and AK-47s and some other things. Much the same as me. Together we will enter the citadel and take the gold. What I need to know is your desires, Captain."

"To break through to the Atlantic," Donovan said.

"And to come and go as we please in the future."

"How will you get through that waterfall?" Patino asked.

"We plan to blow it up, of course. We are on our way now to take a closer look."

"I have not been that close myself, but I hear that it is formidable . . . the wall of a huge bomb crater. Do you have the power to break through?"

"We should."

"Tell me about your ship. I have not heard of *Liberator*."

"She is an advanced nuclear submarine with attack and short-range missile capability," Donovan said. "We are also a research vessel whose new mission is worldwide rescue. Having picked up a distress call from New York, we are on our way to investigate and help out."

"That is very noble," Patino said.

"We think so."

"Some day you may come to Colombia. My farm in Zaragosa is just up the mountain road from Cartagena, and I have heard stories that the suffering there is very great. In this last war the population centers suffered; the rural areas are relatively intact. But there is much disease everywhere."

"What kind of disease?"

"From the fallout, I guess. There is a kind of madness like what we saw in the Central American War, but worse."

"White-shirts," Charlie said.

"Who?" Patino asked.

"The lunatics on the other side of the canal," Donovan said.

"Oh yes, I have heard stories. They are the walking dead, rumors say."

"Close enough. You don't want them to cross over, especially if you have problems of your own."

"Rumors say that madness on our continent has depleted many cities. I have only heard about Cartagena."

"So, radiation psychosis is worldwide, as we suspected," Donovan said.

17

Alex fell asleep a few hours before dawn, sitting on the jungle floor and leaning against the tree stump, her shoulders cradled between Jennings's knees. He had spent the hours forcing himself to stay awake, pointing his weapon out into the night and listening to the periodic howls of whatever-it-was.

With the coming of the new day the howls faded quickly into the jungle, finally disappearing to both sides of the volcano.

Then the daytime sounds of birds and monkeys reappeared and filled the air with a million sounds. The racket was normally unsettling, but this time Jennings welcomed it. It was the sound of normal life in the South Pacific and it was noisy, but none of it was dangerous.

At six A.M. the first of the colonists began to stir. While most slept late on that first full day in their new home, a number rose early, perhaps disbelieving that it was really true. They stretched muscles uncramped for the first time in months, and breathed air free of radiation, or pollution of any kind. The smells in the air were of hibiscus and salt and the sounds were of wild things in nature. Of all those humans that slept on Espiritu that night, only Jennings and Alex had heard the howling from the direction of the volcano.

It was half past six before Jennings got her up. At first Alex jumped up, looking wildly into the jungle for the origin of the howling. But there was nothing there, and quickly she realized that night had passed into day without lethal incident.

"What happened last night?" she asked, wiping her eyes.

"Nothing, thank God," Jennings said.

"Those sounds..."

"The wolves. Or whatever they were. They faded beginning an hour ago. Disappeared around to the other side of the volcano. I think we've heard the last of them for a while."

"What were they?"

"Unknown. At least no one else in the settlement heard them. Look at these people," he said, gesturing at three colonists who were gathering breadfruit. "They're happy. They have the future that none of them expected a while ago."

"We can't let them down," Alex said.

Jennings agreed. "Let's get some breakfast, then take a walk into that jungle and see if we can't find out what we're dealing with."

"Go into the jungle?" she asked, aghast. "Alone?"

"With our weapons. We can hold our own against wolves."

"Hold our own?"

"We'd have a fighting chance. I *am* a pretty good shot, you know."

"You are?" she asked uncertainly.

"Yeah," he replied. "Pretty good."

"We come to what I think you call the 'bottom line,' Captain," Patino said, patting his AK-47. "Will you stand in the way of our attacking the citadel?"

"No, but on one condition," Donovan replied.

"Let's hear it."

"Give us forty-eight hours to blast our way through to the Atlantic."

"That's what you want?"

"We'll blow that dam, wait for the current to stabilize into a passable flow, then sail into the Atlantic.

You can take your gold and as much vengeance as you can stomach, and no one will stop you."

"And you want nothing from this place?"

"We've taken some machine guns. We'll take apart his micronuke before we go."

"That is fine with me. I already have one back on my ranch. But forty-eight hours is a long time, Captain. Especially since those radiation badges you're wearing indicate that your maximum exposure to this place is just a matter of hours. We're no more immune to radiation than you. We planned to be in and out within one day. That will give us more radiation than we would like, but still an acceptable amount. Two days is out of the question."

"One day, then," Donovan said. "Twenty-four hours."

"I will present that to Gital," Patino offered. "If he agrees, we can postpone our attack until . . ." He consulted his watch. "Dawn tomorrow. That will let us get the gold and leave before receiving a lethal dose of radiation."

"Fair enough."

"Our only problem lies in Romanus's vault. If it is as impregnable as we have heard, it could be a whole day to open. That will keep us in the danger zone far too long."

Donovan was astonished. "Don't tell me that you came all this way to break into a bank and didn't bring burglar's tools?"

"Sadly, we lost our best safecracker in the jungle. He strayed from camp and a jaguar got him."

"Jaguar?" Donovan asked, feeling more than a little uncomfortable.

"The wild animals seem to have gone crazy," Patino said. "The jaguars in particular. They are everywhere. I caution you against them. Even close to ground zero they are everywhere."

"Jaguars," Charlie said, echoing his brother. "Seven feet long, four hundred pounds. Nasty disposition to begin with."

"We'll watch out for them," Donovan said. "Chief,

do you think you're up to a little bank robbing?"

"I think it can be arranged," Smith said.

"Are you joking?" Patino said. "You would help us?"

"Give us twenty-four hours and we'll crack that safe for you," Smith said.

"You have a deal," Patino said, shaking Donovan's hand.

The dam was a thick one, made of earth that was thrown up with the force of 100,000 tons of TNT. The crater measured a mile across and this was its southern wall, a massive piling up of dirt, rocks and canal debris over which Pacific Ocean water tumbled with the force of a million Niagaras.

Donovan looked down on it from high ground to the south. From his slightly elevated vantage point, the dam looked like a cold-water nightmare that was keeping *Liberator* at bay.

"I make that to be two hundred yards thick," Smith said, estimating distances and thicknesses on a laser rangefinder.

"The water looks about ten feet deep at the center," Donovan said.

"About ten feet. And running at better than forty knots over the dam. That's enough water flow to erode any hole we punch in the dam. Unfortunately, I don't think we can punch through it with a torpedo."

"Then we'll drop a Mark 97N on it," Donovan said. "One of our tactical nukes will do the job."

"We don't even have to leave our present mooring to do that," Charlie said.

Donovan replied, "As much as you would like to sit on the deck, pop a can of beer and watch the fireworks, we will have to move into midstream and power up. The current will skyrocket once we punch that hole, and there will be whirlpool effects all over the Ciudad Romanus area. It won't be safe at anchor."

"We have to throttle up and fight the current at midstream," Smith said.

Charlie prowled up and down the high ground, shooting footage of the earthen dam and the maelstorm of water pouring over it with the chip camera. Once the images were captured on the videochip, the storage disk could be transferred from camera to playback unit on the ship and fed into the computers for precise measurement of density and flow rates.

He also shot the canal water as it funneled over the dam.

"We'll need a lot of computer analysis of this water to estimate current effects in the canal as a whole," Smith said. "Once this baby blows, it will really be like shooting the rapids."

"The ship will need a little luck," Donovan agreed. "The consolation is that we've been pretty lucky so far."

"Well, let's get going," Smith said. "If we get back to the citadel by noon, I can have the micronuke apart by midnight and stored onboard by dawn."

"Then we can blow this thing and get the fuck outta here," Donovan said.

He led the way back to the Jeeps, which were pulled to the side of the road that led back to Ciudad Romanus. That section of road ran through woods and swamps that alternated in wide bands running deep into the wild. Houses were few and most of the larger trees had been blown over by the force of the blast. Trees were flattened away from ground zero, and in most places only ground scrub under six feet tall stood upright.

That gave the surroundings an unworldly look that was made more so by a moderate wind that rustled the dead leaves and scorched twigs.

Smith was about to turn over the engine of his Jeep when Charlie raised a cautionary hand.

"Hold on a minute," he said, his legendary instincts working overtime.

"What is it?" Donovan asked.

"I'm not sure," Charlie said, raising the Franchi.

"Patino or his men?"

"No . . . not them."

He wandered across the tarmac and to the edge of

a patch of woods where knocked-down trees and scrub edged up against a swamp. He looked into the woods for a long moment, then shrugged and walked back towards the convoy, the muzzle of his rifle in the air.

It was then that the cat struck, leaping from the trunk of a fallen tree and into the air, covering ten yards in its first bound and seven in its second.

"Charlie!" Donovan yelled, and his brother wheeled and fired without aiming, catching the jaguar in the chest and neck with eight slugs.

The animal let out a terrific roar and twisted in midair, crashing to the pavement as Charlie dived out of the way.

There was another movement, down the road a bit. Donovan pulled his Colt and fired at a second animal, smaller than the first but no less vicious.

Charlie fired again and another wild cat died in agony, writhing on the pavement and howling.

"Son of a bitch!" Charlie swore, running for the Jeep and hopping inside.

"It's San Francisco all over again," Smith said, putting the Jeep in gear.

The first animal, seven feet long and with a rich yellow coat spotted with large black rosettes, lay in mid-road with its huge head and neck lying flat and bleeding. The three Jeeps passed by, their guards standing at special alert as the woods and swamps rolled by. Shooting at men was one thing. Men were rational for the most part and predictable even when racked by radiation psychosis, but wolf and jaguar attacks were something no man is ever really prepared for.

All the way back to Ciudad Romanus, Donovan and his men looked from one side to the other constantly, and no one was really sure when another attack might come and from where.

"Jaguars aren't supposed to attack men," Charlie said.

"And timber wolves don't prowl in San Francisco," Donovan said.

Alex said, "Just how good of a shot are you?"

"I never won any medals but get respectable scores on the firing range," Jennings said, a little miffed at having his ability questioned.

"Shoot straight this morning."

"I'll try. Where are you taking us?" he asked.

"This trail is recent and well-traveled. It's also been in use for quite a while. If you look carefully, you'll see that a lot of work went into keeping it clear of growth."

"Where does it go?"

"I'm not sure. I made maps extrapolated from the satellite photographs. One thing for sure is that this trail was plenty important to the natives, because they used it a lot. According to the map, it leads from the settlement inland to the rim of the volcano. From there it breaks in two and heads around the rim, leading to the beach on both north and south shores of the island."

The birds piped down as the strangers moved through the jungle. As they moved inland, eventually they lost contact with the settlement other than by radio, which maintained a link with a transmitter brought ashore from one of the boats.

The trail ran consistently uphill, narrowing as it went, finally reaching a sort of tropical timberline, the demarcation point where jungle vegetation gave way to scrub plants and mosses that grew only on the rocks of the volcano slopes. The volcano towered above them, its spire obscured by low-lying clouds.

The mountain was quiet, but its reputation instilled in them the feeling that it rumbled silently, plotting death and destruction. Looking up the slopes, they could see dark rivulets where molten lava had etched a path downhill, killing as it went. Above a few hundred feet up the slope, everything that dared to grow was regularly burned away.

"I don't know how smart it is living within the shadow of this thing," Jennings said.

"The natives liked it well enough," Alex argued.

"Look what happened to them."

"We don't *know* what happened to them. Anyway, the flow pattern from this volcano is away from the settlement."

"How do you know?"

"From the satellite images. Most of the infrared is on the west side, which is on the opposite side of the island from the settlement. Lava flows that way and ends up in the ocean. The settlement won't get washed away by lava."

"What was the flow pattern on Krakatoa?" Jennings asked, looking warily at the charred rocks uphill.

"You're impossible," Alex said. "Come on, tiger . . . let's check out the north side of the island."

Dr. Fisher worked the CD ROM memory of the diagnostics computer to analyze ionized tissue samples from the white-shirts and other corpses and compare them with records of all the major and minor diseases of man. Everything related to radiation poisoning was examined, including raw data from Hiroshima victims and survivors, natives of Bikini Atoll, U.S. Army volunteers from White Sands in the 1940s and Colombian peasants affected by the nuclear shelling in the Central American War. Data also were included from San Francisco victims and other white-shirts that *Liberator* had encountered in her travels.

"Check this out," Dr. Fisher exclaimed, pointing at a display of data from a tissue sample. "This guy got a dose of five thousand rads: cerebral edema, shock and extreme neurological disturbances, and died within hours. This other one is only three thousand rads, and died in three days."

"They're from Colombia, right?" Donovan said.

"Peru. This one from Colombia had severe vascular damage, loss of fluids and electrolytes into intercellular spaces and the GI tract. He died in ten days."

"The white-shirts we encountered in San Francisco lived for two weeks or more after the war. They must have gotten a lower dose."

Fisher nodded: "This other one is about one thousand rads: bone marrow destruction and demolition of the autoimmune system. Total susceptibility to infection. He died in five weeks. Some of these least-severe cases can linger indefinitely. Sometimes for years."

"We know now that white-shirts can last for three months," Donovan said.

"And they still have necrosis all over the body. Why that doesn't simply eat them up eludes me. But it's the neurological damage that's the real puzzle."

"The psychotic symptoms are common to all of them."

"Yeah, and the symptoms are still symbiotic. The rage justifies the physical deterioration and vice versa. In masses they're *strong*. The biological symptoms are in league with purely psychological ones. There still must be a biological cause underlying the insanity. I don't know if I'm getting any closer."

Donovan said, "You have to do it. If there's a biological cause there could be a biological cure. We could save some of these people."

"Well, the ROM diagnostics have come through for me. You remember that some time ago I found a connection with the data assembled during the Central American War?"

"Vividly."

"In my research I found a connection with AIDS. The HIV virus was neurotropic—it attacked nerve cells. In the terminal stage it attacked the sectors of the brain responsible for cognition. Psychosis often resulted, and psychosis of a type remarkably like what we see in the white-shirts. The development of the AIDS vaccine pretty much ended that plague, but a similarly neurotropic virus mutated during the Central American War in the Andes—about the only region in the world where AIDS inoculations weren't made.

"I felt pretty sure that the radiation spread in that war caused the AIDS virus to mutate, and to attack those sectors of the brain that control aggression."

"What about the means of transmission?" Donovan asked.

"I have ruled out airborne and casual contact. It isn't a contact virus either. In fact, judging by the fact we have discovered no new victims and that the war is three months in the past, I would say that there *are* no new victims and that the war's radiation was the solitary cause. The worst-off white-shirts will die and, with more research and some luck, I'll have a way of treating the less severe cases."

"Like Jake and Lisa," Donovan said, referring to the two teenagers they picked up in San Francisco and transferred to the *Mayflower II* for safekeeping until a cure was found.

"I feel confident I can help them," Dr. Fisher said. "But the vast majority of white-shirts will die, especially the more aggressive ones."

"How soon?" Donovan asked.

"Not soon enough to let you take a stroll on the far bank of the canal. However, there may be an up side to this plague."

"I consider myself a creative man and I fail to find one," Donovan said.

"The white-shirts are *very strong*. Most of them should in fact be dead and lying in the grave. Remember that one whose face you quite literally punched in? I don't know what kept him on his feet. I don't know what keeps any of them on their feet, but I sure would like to."

"Adrenaline?"

"Maybe five percent of it is adrenaline. The rest of that strength is unknown. If I can find the cause I might have a potent drug to cure serious ills or prolong life. I will need a lot of time for research, and more bodies."

"You sound like Frankenstein, Doctor," Donovan said. "His subject was strong, too."

The captain left the subbasement and rode the elevator to the lobby, where he found Chief Smith in the power room with several of his technicians. The MicroScale Home Nuclear Unit was surrounded by floodlights that illuminated every crack in the device, which was a lot smaller than Donovan imagined.

Since they were designed for home or estate use, the compact nuclear units were built in modular fashion. Their components stacked much like an old-fashioned stereo component system, with a minimum of wires and tubing. The thermopile, which converted the reactor's heat into electricity for powering home systems, was contained in a black box the size of a large suitcase and might even be mistaken *for* a suitcase were it not for the extreme weight—about 2,500 pounds.

The nuclear furnace itself was more a workshop than a conventional nuclear pile. The neosteel rods impregnated with uranium polymers made clean heat with no by-products and lent themselves to encasement in another black module, this one more the size of a trunk and weighing more than 10,000 pounds.

Since the heat transfer was done electronically and through implanted-chip monitoring, there was almost no chance of catastrophic failure. Coolant pump failure, that old bugaboo of conventional nuclear plants, was impossible, since there was no coolant to fail. The only failure existed upon depletion of the fuel, and that was estimated to occur in no fewer than forty years. Since the first micronukes were only test-marketed in 2005, there was no expectation of failure much before the middle of the century.

"The only problem is the weight of the thing," Chief Smith said, surveying the project and wiping his brow.

"The largest module is how big?" Donovan asked.

"Ten thousand pounds."

"How are you going to transport it to the ship?"

"Forklift from here through the lobby and out the front wall. Once we get it on the dock there's no choice—we'll have to dock the ship."

"I know. I don't like it."

"No other way to get ten thousand pounds on board," Smith said. "We have to bring her in broadside to dock, extend the equipment crane, and lower the modules into the aft hold."

"How long will we have to stay docked?" Donovan asked.

"Three hours . . . maybe five."

"We'll be vulnerable that whole time. Romanus can get at us. So can Patino and Gital."

"But those guys are fighting each other," Smith protested.

"So they say. I hear a lot of talk about revenge, gold, and doing things for the sake of future generations, but so far all I see is two armed camps—one outside the wall of the citadel and the other across the swamp. There may or may not be a third armed camp off to the west. The bottom line is they ain't firing at each other and are always available to fire on us."

"What for? The ship?"

"*Liberator* is a ticket out of this hole," Donovan said.

"But things aren't so bad in the Andes, according to Patino."

"So he says. If things aren't so bad in South America, how come we don't pick up any radio? I'm not talking about fifty-thousand-watt FM stations, now. I mean police radios and walkie-talkies. We can hear just about anything they put on the air, and so far it ain't been a thing."

"We *did* pick up Alex on a police radio from on top of the Golden Gate Bridge . . ."

"When we were far out at sea. You get my point?"

"I get it," Smith said grimly. "If there are a lot of survivors in South America, how come they ain't makin' some noise? I'll see if I can't load the micronuke on board in under three hours."

"Good. What time do you want the ship to come in?"

"It's oh-nine-hundred now and we have a good six hours' work ahead of us just to take this thing apart and haul it out onto the dock. I'll need the ship at around..." He checked his watch and said, "Fifteen hundred hours."

"I'll go break the news to Romanus," Donovan said.

"Break what news?"

"That we're stealing his power plant."

"First you take my machine guns and now you want my power plant?" Romanus thundered.

"You won't need either," Donovan said, matter-of-factly. "Your food is almost gone and the water is running radioactive. There are two armies of huns at the gate. You have no choice but to leave as quickly as possible."

"Where will I go?"

"To the Andes."

"But the mountains are in the hands of my enemies."

"Bribe them," Donovan said. "It's a time-honored custom. And you have more gold than you can ever use."

"What of the shipload of cocaine in my harbor?"

"I had it checked out. It's melted down, Romanus. It's sludge and should be in a sewer. You made your citadel blastproof but not your harbor. All you have left to bargain with is the gold. That seems to have value to Patino, who thinks that his children will live long enough to see it revalued."

"Patino wants to kill me," Romanus said.

"Make it a big bribe. Split the take with Patino and Gital in exchange for your life. Go with them to the mountains. There's nothing left here but death. Take your men and start new lives. For God's sake, man, the whole world is barely alive. Another week here and the radioactivity will have melted down your genes."

"I can stay in my citadel. That is safe."

"Until the food runs out and the water kills you. Chief Smith inspected your automation system. It can keep out everything but polluted groundwater."

"Then I will die fighting. Like a man."

"That's it, isn't it? It's a macho thing that makes no sense. You want to die because you're in a kind of Alamo mentality. You think that history will remember you more kindly if you die fighting. Well, wise up. History ended three months ago. This is fantasy."

Romanus shook his head and sank sadly down into one of the chairs on the observation deck. Mendosa made him a gin and orange juice and rested the glass lightly in his hands. The general sipped it disinterestedly.

"How much time do I have?" he asked.

"The micronuke comes out at three this afternoon. You will have battery power for three days. That will give you plenty of time to negotiate with Patino and Gital and split."

"They will kill me and take my gold anyway."

"I'll negotiate," Donovan said. "If I can't make them see the light, I have a whole bunch of missiles that can."

Mendosa said, "After you've been nuked once you start to lose your fear of it."

"You have no choice," Donovan said.

From the other room, Charlie called his name and even Percy beckoned him into the radio room. There the two men sat at the main console, huddling over a scanning transceiver as if it were the secret of life itself.

"Did you pick up something?" Donovan asked.

"Yeah. I got New York," Charlie said proudly. "I think it's the same guy that Jennings picked up."

A voice came through, broken up by static but not nearly as badly as the first time he was heard, in Papeete harbor. He said, "Calling CQ from New York. Sheepshead Bay. I have battery power for two hours tonight."

"*'Tonight'* he said," Donovan whispered. "This must be a regular broadcast."

"This is New York calling for anyone who can respond. Please respond. I know there's someone out there."

"Can I talk to him?" Donovan asked.

Charlie handed over the microphone.

"New York, this is the U.S.S. *Liberator* calling. Do you copy?"

The voice hesitated, shocked, then came back choked with emotion: "New York ... I mean *Liberator* ... where are you? Who are you? I can't believe I finally got someone."

Donovan could hear the sounds of celebration in the background. That sound—laughter and something like joy—came across the thousands of miles like a long overdue beacon of hope.

"This is Tom Donovan commanding the nuclear submarine *Liberator*. How do you copy?"

"We read you fine, Captain. Where are you?"

"In Panama trying to break through into the Atlantic to rescue you. The canal is blocked but we may be able to unblock it. What's your name? How many are you?"

"My name is Sal. There are ten of us. Two families. I got a party fishing boat. I mean I *had* a party fishing boat. My buddy Pete worked her with me. That was until the war. I mean, there *was* a war, right?"

"Right," Donovan said.

"We saw New York go up. There was this light and then nothing. A lot of wind and the seas picked up. We slept for a long time. Hid longer. Then the crazies came after a few days or a week."

"I know. They're all over the place. We call them white-shirts."

"They're wearing white here too," Sal said. "It's weird. But the war opened up the bay. We're an island now, separated from the mainland of the city. The crazies rule the inland."

"They can't swim," Donovan reported.

"We're okay here. We catch fish and the water is all right. I mean, I *think* it's all right. When can you get here?"

"A week or ten days if we can break through to the Atlantic. Indefinitely longer if we can't."

"Are there many survivors on your side of the world?"

"We just transported sixty-seven from San Francisco to the South Pacific. We're starting a new world of our own. You're welcome to join us. We especially need guys that know how to fish."

"That's Pete and me. My God, Captain, you don't know how good it is to hear your voice."

"You don't know how good it is to hear yours. I grew up in New York. In the city. Manhattan."

"Sorry, Captain. That's all gone now. I think so, anyway. It's hard to tell anything from this island."

"Can you see any other survivors?"

"Only white-shirts. We're too busy and too scared to go exploring. It's enough work to catch fish and keep the batteries charged."

"How do you do that?"

"We set up a small windmill using an old airplane prop and the generator from my boat. It works pretty good. But I got to get off now. This radio uses a lot of juice."

"Understood. How will we find you?"

"Just come up Ambrose Channel and hook a right past Breezy Point. We're holed up in the clock tower of the old college building. You can't miss us. We got the only windmill in this part of town."

"Keep listening on this frequency and we'll see you as soon as we can. *Liberator* out."

"Wow," Charlie said, whistling between his teeth.

Donovan was swollen with pride. "Our mission, gentlemen . . . to find and rescue guys like Sal and Pete and their families."

"You made a believer out of me," Percy agreed.

The north trail snaked around the base of the volcano, hugging the mountain for the first two miles before turning away, toward the sea. As the day wore on, Alex and Jennings hiked farther and farther into the jungle, keeping the volcano on the left and walking through miles and miles of foliage so thick even air had a hard time passing through it.

The trail was like all the others: man-made but not used in a few months. At the noon hour, they stopped in a glen where the path widened and gave way to a patch of sunlit grass and moss. They picked fruit and sat on the grass to have lunch and listen to the birds, which were afraid and silent at first, then got used to the human presence and let go a fusillade of amusing whistles.

After six hours of roaming the Espiritu wilderness in search of timber wolves, Alex and Jennings had found nothing more sinister than tropical birds and the occasional lizard. The howling they heard at night was only a memory, and a fading one at that. As terrifying as it seemed in the dead of night, in the light of the jungle noon, surrounded by plants and animals and vulnerable to anything that nature wanted to throw at them, Alex and Jennings felt safe.

Maybe what they heard was simply the product of an overtired imagination. Maybe it was gone, never to return.

At one in the afternoon they continued on, pushing to the north side of the volcano and emerging, finally, on the north beach.

Unlike the other beaches they had seen, this one was unused by the natives. There were no pirogues—no boats or nets at all, and this despite the calm, shallow sea and lack of breakers.

Jennings looked out to sea, a bit confused.

"No native boats. Yet this looks like an ideal spot to launch boats and fish."

"Maybe there are sharks," Alex said.

"There are sharks everywhere, especially since the war. We found them all across the Pacific, even at depth. There will be a lot all around this island. Be glad we have the lagoon."

"I'm hot for a swim, but not that hot."

"Maybe this is too far from the settlement for the natives to use as a beach," Jennings said.

"That doesn't make sense either. The natives could use *all* this island for settlement. Okay, maybe not the part beneath the lava flow, but the rest of it. Surely this north section, especially since it's easy to launch boats here. It doesn't make sense that they'd only use one part, by the lagoon. Unless . . ."

"Unless . . ."

"There's some reason they *can't* use the rest of the island."

Jennings asked, "Would that reason have something to do with wolves?"

"Maybe. Not wolves, of course. But *something* that goes bump in the night."

"There could be a religious reason. Maybe this part of the island is taboo."

"All I know is there has to be a reason the natives stayed in the settlement," Alex said.

Jennings shrugged and walked away from the sea, and had only gotten a few strides along the beach when he saw the footprints.

There were only a few at first, then a few turned to many and soon cut a path from the low-water mark up to the jungle, where they disappeared into a thicket.

"Look at this," Jennings said.

"I see. How many men would you say made those prints?"

"I'm no Indian scout. It could be a dozen. Then again, it could be one man with a healthy appetite for walking. But it's not the number of prints that worries me. It's the location."

"Where? On the beach?"

"Down to the low-water mark," Jennings said.

"Oh," she replied, realizing the significance.

"Those prints were made within the past six hours, probably less."

Alex looked at him and then her eyes followed the trail of footprints until it disappeared into the jungle.

The two of them walked in the footprints up to the jungle, then pulled aside palm fronds to peer into the thick foliage. The prints led into a thicket of dense jungle foliage that had no trail.

"Maybe I'll take a swim after all," she said.

The projectile was launched from the woodlands to the south and west of Ciudad Romanus. It soared up over the swamp and the road approaching from the west and impacted at the base of the Great Hall of the People, shattering the deadly calm afternoon air as it sent up a shower of flagstone fragments from the paved walk.

"Grenade!" one of Donovan's men yelled.

"More incoming," another warned as a brace of missiles landed, one detonating harmlessly on the rear wall of the Great Hall of the People but the other landing perilously close to machine gun emplacement number one.

Up in the radio room, Donovan got the word on his transceiver: "We're under attack, Captain," Hooper called. "Incoming grenades from the wooded area to the southwest."

"Gital," Romanus swore.

"The one who promised nothing," Donovan snarled.

"I *told* you these men could not be trusted. Now will you believe me?"

"Now will you get your men up fighting? Manning those machine guns would be a start."

"But to do that I will have to let them into the citadel!"

"Can you fire six machine guns yourself? Get a move on it, Romanus."

"I will handle it personally," Mendosa swore.

"Good fellow. We'll guard the approach from the

canal side. Mr. Percy, move the small arms party onto the promenade."

Charlie said, "Begging my brother's pardon, but I *am* Chief Gunnery Officer."

"Get a move on," Donovan said, and then Charlie and Percy were off in the direction of the elevator, and Mendosa was right behind.

Romanus and Donovan went back to the observation room, and from there could see several squads of men progressing up the road from the west, pausing now and again to launch a 40-mm grenade from a shoulder mount.

"Gital is a selfish man," Romanus said. "He has opened fire, hoping to get all the gold for himself. Now Patino will have to do likewise."

"Any chance these two assholes will kill each other?" Donovan asked, hoping beyond hope.

"Not much of one."

"Damn, I thought I could avoid this."

"Thinking that you can negotiate your way out of every crisis is a mind-set more common to Europeans," Romanus said. "You are an American."

As he spoke, two mortar rounds crashed against the spire. They came from the east, from Patino's direction.

"Idiots," Donovan said, and went downstairs to fight.

Mendosa opened the gates long enough to admit his men, who fled into the hallowed hall so eagerly that you would barely know they had come to fight for a man they despised. They brought AK-47s and M16s and twelve of them took up the machine gun positions—six to fire and six to load. The men with the submachine guns overturned benches and took up firing positions behind them, laying down a withering fire.

The citadel's blastproofing was designed to withstand low-frequency disturbances, which is to say, shock waves from nearby major explosions. It was less effective against small arms, and rows of bullet holes soon appeared in the lower floors of the three citadel buildings.

The grenade and mortar launches continued for a few minutes and took a modest toll—one machine gun was temporarily put out of commission as its gunner and ammo man were cut down by shrapnel. But they were replaced, and the mount was soon back in action.

After that the mortars and grenades stopped. There was no cover on the road, and fire from Mendosa's machine guns made standing in the open hazardous to the health.

Twenty minutes after it began, the attack stopped. The fire forced the attackers into the rubble of the old living quarters, where they found shelter among the blown-down and partly burned buildings amidst the rotting corpses of victims of the war. The road was littered with bodies: eight from Patino's group and eleven from Gital's. Only two of Mendosa's men were dead. The first skirmish had been decided in favor of the defenders.

They let out whoops of victory. Mendosa strode proudly across the pavement to where Donovan stood at the south portal to the spire.

"Round one is ours," he said proudly.

"That was well done, Mendosa."

"They will be back as soon as they realize how rotten it is living with corpses. They will come out and fight rather than inhale that stink. And then we will finish them."

"Where's your boss?" Donovan asked, looking around for Romanus.

"He will never come out of his castle," Mendosa said. "He is like Count Dracula—a prisoner of his own fortress. He will remain in there until he starves or poisons himself with the water."

"It may already be too late for him," Dr. Fisher said, making a cautious appearance out of his temporary morgue.

"Good morning, Doctor. Come up for more corpses?"

"I have enough for today, thank you. Are you done shaking the building? If I thought I was going into battle . . ."

"You're in the Navy now, Doctor. Death is what we do. Why don't you go back to the ship and run your results through the computer?"

"My thought exactly," Dr. Fisher said, then headed for the dock.

"So, Colonel, what now? Are you also going to stay here and be killed?"

"No, but I do not think I can negotiate with my adversaries. And I know I can't buy you."

"What then?"

Mendosa tossed up his hands and said, "An appeal to your humanity?"

"We're doing exactly what I said—breaking through to the Atlantic as part of our continuing efforts to rescue survivors of the war. Do you want to be part of that?"

"Like I said, you will need jungle fighters."

"Well, we *are* making our home on a jungle island in the South Pacific. We could use some men who are experienced at jungle living, if not fighting."

"Count me in. And if you can take them, I can find others. There are four officers who are very good. And you can trust them."

"We're leaving as soon as the micronuke is loaded on board," Donovan said. "We're taking no gold."

"There's no place to spend it in the South Pacific anyway," Mendosa said.

"Welcome aboard, Colonel Mendosa," Donovan said, shaking the man's hand. "Can you and your men hold off the attackers for the rest of the day?"

"As the saying goes, it is a piece of cake," Mendosa said with a smile.

Alex and Jennings continued along the trail around the north side of the volcano, treading a bit more uneasily than they had.

Finding traces of the natives, even of large numbers of natives, would have been comforting. It would have meant that they had seen the colonists' ships and gone into hiding. Nothing more sinister than that. But one man, a man seemingly able to walk through thick jungle foliage without the need of a trail, seemed unsettling.

It was still unsettling when the tracks turned onto a path briefly. From that point on, signs of increasing trail use came to be clear. Feet had trampled the new growth on the trail just enough to suggest that one man passed through on a regular basis.

"Who the hell is this guy?" Alex asked.

"I don't know, but if he answers to 'Friday' I'm going home," Jennings replied.

The trail skimmed the beach for several miles, then turned inland as it rounded the far side of the volcano. The jungle began to thin then as the ground turned acidic and black from soot and lava. On the far western side of the island the land was nearly bare. Sulphurous volcanic soil coated lava flows only recently solidified. A few mosses and lichens grew. But apart from them the landscape was like that of Mars.

They walked cautiously across it, their eyes suddenly hurting from the brilliant sunlight of afternoon and their eyes smarting from the sulphur.

"This is not the paradise part of the island," Alex said.

"No shit. They left this off the travel brochures."

"Whoever our man is, we lost him. His trail stops at the beginning of the lava field."

"There's another way of looking at it. He lost us."

The lava field was two miles wide, and by the time they walked across it they were nearly blinded from the brilliant sun. The jungle resumed as they headed toward the south side of the island. Greenery came back in fits and starts, first as low growth and then as the lush foliage they knew from the land around the settlement.

Wearily pushing through a screen of branches, they found the man who had laid the trail they had lost. Standing in a clearing near the resumption of the trail, they saw him. He was tall, muscular, and tanned, his face bearded and shaded with a battered felt hat over sandy hair. He was about fifty, shirtless, and wearing old khaki trousers that were cut off at the knees.

He stared them down. Alex and Jennings tried to focus their tired eyes on the tall Occidental who it was suddenly clear had led them across the open lava field so he could get a good look at them.

"Baltimore Jack," he said.

"What?" Alex asked.

"I'm Jack, from Baltimore. Who are you?"

"Alex Fisher, from San Francisco."

"Dave Jennings, New Jersey."

"Welcome to my island," he said.

The shelling resumed just after three in the afternoon. The armies of Patino and Gital indeed had enough of the stench in the festering trenches behind the citadel and decided upon another assault.

The attack opened with the expected burst of mortars and grenades. But this time there was a difference. The shelling came from dug-in positions at the periphery of the rubble from which they could lob shells without much chance of being hit by machine gun fire.

Mendosa was as good as Donovan hoped. He sheltered his machine gun positions and took the shelling without wasting valuable ammunition firing at rubble. The bet was that he could withstand the shelling and that the troops out in the field, who were about as far from being mechanized as it was possible to be in the twenty-first century, would soon run out of mortars and grenades.

Adhering to his tight schedule, Chief Smith pulled the micronuke and used one of the citadel's forklifts to carry the modular components out to the promenade. There, Charlie's men stood guard with Franchis ready to fire both from the promenade and the deck of *Liberator*, which Donovan brought to dock at three.

Tied securely with her port side to the dock, *Liberator* turned swiftly into a crude approximation of a cargo carrier. Her equipment crane sprouted from the aft deck and reached up just far enough to pluck the strapped-up components from the promenade and lower them into the hold, which was designed into the ship as a portal for replacement engine parts. The forward torpedo and missile hold had a crane that was too light and specialized for heavy lifting of a general sort.

By five in the afternoon the loading was done. Donovan emitted a huge sigh of relief as *Liberator* moved away from the besieged city and returned to her offshore anchorage. With the micronuke safely stored and the captured Walther PB AutoStrafes set up on deck to guard the promenade, all that remained was to blow the dam and weather the storm of water that would cascade down the canal afterwards.

Before they could do that, they had to retrieve Mendosa and his four men, who remained holding down the fort against the attackers. Charlie Donovan had joined them too, for his marksmanship was as good as his intuition and it was impossible to keep him out of a fight.

Donovan assigned Percy and Smith to get on the computer and work out all the details of blowing the dam. How much explosive and where? Missile or torpedo? What was the projected depth after breakthrough? What was the projected current flow? And how fast would *Liberator* have to be moving upstream in order to avoid being carried backwards? Then he armed himself with a Franchi and some extra ammo and had himself transported ashore to collect his brother.

He thought it would be a short trip.

Baltimore Jack led Alex and Jennings down the path to where it rejoined the beach, this time on the western shore of the island. On their right lay a stretch of shallow sea where years of accumulated lava had built up a plateau. On the left was the deep ocean to the south of Espiritu. At mid-afternoon on that summer day it was flat and clear, with only a few cumulus clouds on the horizon and nothing other than birds near land.

The tall man sat them down on mats that had been woven from palm fronds and dried in the sun, and offered them coconut milk and mangoes. He said, "I have been watching you since you came ashore yesterday."

"And you wanted to see if we were dangerous or not," Alex said.

"Yeah, and I wanted to see how good you are at living in the jungle."

"Well?"

"Not very good. But you're new."

"We learn fast," Alex said. "Tell me . . . what do you prefer to be called? Baltimore or Jack?"

"Baltimore. Until we get to know each other better let's be formal."

"Okay, Baltimore . . . what do you mean, *your* island?"

"It's mine. I bought it a year ago. Don't tell me you don't know who I am."

"I don't know who you are. Do you, Dave?"

Jennings shook his head. "There's something familiar about you, though."

"You never heard of Baltimore Jack, WWF champion from 1997 through 2006?"

"What's WWF?" Alex asked.

Jennings shook his head and groaned. "World Wrestling Federation. Now I remember."

"You're a professional wrestler?" Alex asked.

"Undisputed champion of the world for the decade spanning the millennium," the man said proudly.

"Didn't you kill somebody?" Jennings asked.

"Well, there *was* that little problem. I was hooked up in the first Russian-American professional wrestling tournament. The Russian champ was this big guy from out east—they billed him as the Siberian Tiger. Our match was the top of the card at the new Gorbachev Exposition Hall in Red Square—a really big deal that was supposed to inaugurate a new era of pro sports in the Soviet Union. You remember, Jennings."

"I sure do. It was the year the National Football League opened an expansion team in Leningrad."

"And you killed the guy?" Alex asked.

"It wasn't *my* idea to slam him on his head," Jack said, rather defensively. "And I would never have done it if they had told me he couldn't take a full-weight head slam. So . . . the publicity was all bad and I thought it best to retire."

"You took your money and bought this island," Jennings said.

"That's it. All my wrestling money went into this place. I always was kind of a loner. You know, when you have the rep as a killer not that many people want to be your pal. I decided to go somewhere where nobody knew who I was. And I always had this romantic notion of the South Pacific."

"What happened to the natives?" Alex asked.

"They found out who I was," Jack said, a bit ruefully. "Some left . . . others were easy to buy out. I paid for their resettlement on Tahiti, which was in need of plenty of hands for the new mining venture. I moved here a year ago and for the past six months I've been alone."

"All alone?"

"It's not so bad. Every three months the boat comes from Papeete."

"Not anymore," Jennings said.

"Why not? I mean, the boat is a week overdue, but that's not unusual."

"The boat isn't coming," Alex said.

"Papeete is deserted," Jennings added.

"You mean you don't know?" she said. "The sky didn't turn dark or anything?"

"What the hell are you talking about?" Jack asked.

"We've had World War Three," Alex said. "The world as we knew it is over."

21

Donovan caught up with his brother during a lull in the fighting.

Charlie was with Mendosa, who had erected a command post of sorts from turned-over benches that had been augmented with oil drums brought up from the loading dock. From behind it they had a commanding view of the rubble-strewn living quarters behind the citadel, from which still came occasional shots.

At four in the afternoon a strange quiet had fallen over the battleground. For nearly an hour that peace had prevailed, giving the unwary the impression that the fighting was over.

Knowing better, Charlie and Mendosa inspected their troops, which now had dwindled to twenty due to four deaths, eight injuries, and a number of defections. More than two dozen men had fled into the jungle, either to join the enemy or make a possibly hopeless run for an elusive safety.

When Donovan caught up with the remaining defenders they were at the southeast corner of the citadel, overlooking the road that wound down the canal to the rubble of Panama City. The city wall was less formidable there, not so high off the ground, and circular steel stairs wound down to the side of the road. Around the corner and near a ramp leading to the other entrance to the underground of the citadel stood the Jeep that Donovan had taken out to Gatun for the inspection.

A solitary machine gun emplacement stood on the rampart corner, where it could sweep the road as well as the arm of the jungle that came right up to the lip of the pavement.

Donovan said, "The cargo has been loaded onto the ship and we're ready to sail. Assemble the men you want to take and we'll go."

Charlie asked, "Did Percy make the calculations for blowing the dam?"

"He's doing it now. In my opinion, a missile detonation at ground level will rupture the dam, and if we're heading upstream at thirty knots when it cuts loose we'll be safe."

"That doesn't sound too hard."

"Not everything we do has to be a trial."

"Have you heard anything from Patino and Gital?"

"A while ago they appeared to be arranging a meeting. There was some vaguely coded talk on the radio as well as a lot of movement on the jungle line there, across the swamp."

He pointed out an area a mile away which was relatively dry yet free of dense foliage. Several figures were standing around there, and there was what looked like a Jeep.

"That whole area is permeated with dirt roads," Mendosa said. "Half of them aren't passable and it's hard to know which are. I know the land well, but it's impossible to go out there right now."

"Maybe I can give reason one more shot," Donovan said.

"Do you want to try talking to Patino again?" Mendosa asked.

"I don't see what harm it could do. Let me try."

Donovan brought the transceiver to his lips, and said, "Patino, this is Donovan. Are you guys tired of being shot at yet?"

The reply came back swiftly. "Captain . . . you are still alive. How is that possible?"

"It was a snap. Now, answer my question—what good is this killing doing either of us?"

"My partner, Señor Gital, is not as trusting as I am. He thinks that you intend to steal the gold for yourself."

"Is his foolishness sufficient reason to get yourself killed?" Donovan asked.

"I like you, Captain. You are an intelligent man. Leave now with your ship and your life."

"I'll leave when I get ready. Let's make another deal—stop shooting for a few hours and we'll leave the safe door open for you."

"Why would you do that?" Patino asked.

"For your health," Donovan said. "You know very well that the radioactivity in this part of the world is killing you. Stay another day or two and there will be no children to inherit the gold. Leave in a few hours and all will be well."

"I ask again . . . why do you care?"

Donovan said, "You are a wise and powerful man. I may need an ally in South America in the future. I want you to be healthy so you can return the favor when I return to do rescue missions on your continent."

Charlie said, "Wise and powerful?"

"A little bullshit never hurts," Donovan confided.

Patino replied, "I will speak with Gital and get back to you."

"Let's hear it for bullshit," Charlie said.

Baltimore Jack fell into a pensive mood once the reality sank in. His naturally ebullient personality turned dark and somber for a while, but in all he took the news well.

The world was, after all, something he had given up voluntarily the year before. He had sold all his possessions and moved to an island in the South Pacific, there to live in solitude and forget the troubles that civilization had heaped upon him.

The word that the world had been blown away gave him some pensive moments, but he got over them within half an hour.

"Now that it's all over out there, I guess I have no more to fear from it," he said at last.

"Did you really intend to spend the rest of your life alone?" Alex asked.

"I can't answer that question. I thought for a long time that I did. But then, Papeete was only a boat ride away. Finding people was always a possibility. When I bought out the natives I knew that civilization was a distance away, but reachable."

"How did you manage to buy off the natives?" Jennings asked. "That sounds pretty extraordinary."

"Not really. They had formed a co-op and were trying to find a buyer, much the way the guys on Bora-Bora sold land to Dino de Laurentis. It was a real estate transaction, pure and simple. If I bought an island in the Florida Keys you wouldn't think it odd."

"The man has a point," Jennings said, getting up off his mat and stretching.

"So you're here," Jack said, also standing and helping Alex to her feet. "What are your intentions?"

"We'd like to stay. But if that's not possible..."

"No. I heard your story and would like to help. Maybe I'm not cut out for running around the world in a nuclear submarine, but I can help you build a new society. I know this island like the back of my hand. Stay, by all means. Come, let me show you my house."

"House?"

"Sure. You don't think I'm living in a thatched hut, do you?"

"We are."

"I'll show you how to make it more comfortable. Come to my place. It will be dark in a few hours, and you'll never make it back to the settlement in time. Tonight you'll stay with me. I can even offer you a hot shower and a soft bed."

"Accepted," Alex said with a laugh.

Romanus had been plucked from his spire-top hideout and brought down to face his enemies. Donovan did it personally, but only after extracting from Patino the promise to take the old dictator south to the relative safety of the Andes. Romanus would live out the remainder of his days a poor but safe man, taken from the radioactive death of his homeland.

The Tobler Magna safe was the latest model, which included a top-entry door built into the ground level of the Great Hall of the People. After breaking into the Great Hall, Donovan escorted Romanus to the safe entry, where Chief Smith and his technicians were readying to turn the latest electronic diagnostic gear into sophisticated safecracking tools.

X-ray scanners used to detect anomalies in nuclear tubing took pictures of the lock mechanism (Romanus had, as his final defiance, refused to turn over the combination to his enemies). A field-grade computer analyzed the mechanism and provided the coordinates for the laser picks that would disassemble the lock without so much as scratching it.

The job took less than an hour. By seven in the evening, an hour before sundown, the job was done and the door swung open. As Patino and Gital leaned forward in joy and anticipation, the internal lights went on to reveal a room the walls of which were stacked with gleaming gold bars.

Even Charlie was impressed. "My God, is that what Fort Knox looks like?" he exclaimed.

Patino and Gital swept into the vault, pulling out massively heavy ingots and tossing them around like toys.

Donovan smiled. It was like watching children on Christmas morning.

"Enjoy this moment, gentlemen," he said.

Patino said, "You are a man of your word, Captain, and I salute you. Would you change your mind and take some gold as a memento of this occasion?"

"No thanks."

"And you, Mendosa, you old jungle rat! Would you like a gold bar to give your children?"

"Not me. I'm going with Captain Donovan."

"What a shame," Patino said. "We will just have to take it all."

"How will you get it back to Colombia?" Donovan asked.

"I have many trucks on the other side of the swamp. We will manage. And we will look after your radiation-sick dictator. I promise you that he will live as long as his illness lets him."

"I like happy endings," Donovan said. "We'll be getting on our way."

"Wait a minute," said Dr. Fisher, pushing his way into the vault.

"What's the matter?"

"Nobody's going anywhere with anything until I check it out."

"For what?" Patino asked.

"Radiation," the doctor said, using his EnviroTester to check the gold ingot that Patino was holding.

"Where? In the safe?"

"Radiation has a particular affinity for gold," Dr. Fisher said. "Didn't you guys see *Goldfinger*?"

"No."

The doctor checked gold at random around the room, then announced somberly, "Sorry, guys. But this stuff is hot. The whole load of it."

"You mean this gold is radioactive?" Patino said, stunned.

"Yeah. And it will be too hot to handle for at least twenty-five thousand years. You better put down that ingot before your skin starts to peel off."

Patino dropped the ingot, which crashed to the vault floor with a soft *whump*.

Romanus, who had been quiet, suddenly let out a shriek of devilish laughter. "The vault was built below the blastproofing! I never thought to protect the *gold* from radiation! Only myself!"

"You *idiot*!" Patino yelled, whipping out an automatic and emptying the clip into the aging dictator.

"Charlie!" Donovan yelled, and his brother raised his Franchi and drilled Patino with half a dozen rounds.

As the bearded warrior was slammed against the wall of gold and then dropped down to the floor, Gital tore out of the room and down the hall to the outside and freedom. Mendosa was after him in a flash, and so were the others, who were desperate to keep the already paranoid commander from reaching his troops.

Too late. Gital was too far ahead to stop before he ran out of the Great Hall and into a waiting Jeep. All the satisfaction Mendosa got was to get off a few shots at the retreating vehicle before it disappeared back in the direction of the enemy encampment.

"This don't look good," Charlie commented.

The sound shook the Great Hall and startled the men standing behind it.

Off in the woods to the south, light or medium artillery had fired. The smoke puffed through the palm trees. Charlie and Donovan ducked instinctively, expecting the round to be aimed at them. They were disappointed.

Instead, they heard Percy's voice on the radio, saying: "Captain, we're under attack. An artillery round just exploded in the water off the starboard bow. I can't tell where the fire is coming from."

"Dammit, Gital has brought up an artillery piece and is firing on the ship!"

"Where'd he get that?"

"What difference does it make? The ship isn't built to withstand direct hits! Even a light artillery shell could damage us, perhaps beyond our ability to repair at this time!"

As he spoke, another puff of smoke signaled the firing of another round. Soon Percy said, "Another miss, Captain! Off the port bow! He has us bracketed!"

"Get out of there, Mr. Percy! Get my ship to safety!"

"Captain, I won't leave you behind."

"That's an order! We'll be all right."

"I'm taking *Liberator* to mid-channel," Percy said. "Stay on this channel, Captain. We'll arrange a pickup later."

As he spoke, two mortar shells crashed into the Great Hall, sending the defenders diving for cover. Rifle-launched grenades exploded on the ramparts, knocking out two machine gun emplacements and killing the crews. Donovan and his brother started into the Great Hall, then realized that it was a radioactive death trap and ran down the side of the building toward where they left their Jeep.

Mendosa was right with them, yelling, "The citadel is no longer safe for us. The automated defenses and shields cannot hold more than fifteen minutes on battery power."

"Where can we go?" Donovan asked.

"I know a place . . . a stone church ten miles to the southeast . . . on the road to Panama City. We can take refuge there until the ship can pick us up."

"Does Gital know about this church?" Charlie asked, then hit the dirt as a howitzer round crashed nearby, ripping chunks out of the paving.

"No time to worry," Donovan said, running down the steps to the Jeep.

The others piled in behind him, and Donovan put the engine in gear and roared off down the road, a mortar round landing behind them and blasting the tarmac where the vehicle stood the moment before.

The road to Panama City was well traveled for a new road. It was slick from tire rubber and crankcase oil left behind from the many round-trips that Romanus and his entourage made between the capital city and the citadel. To the left was the jungle, which encroached on the road all the more as the distance increased between them and Ciudad Romanus. To the right were dwindling reminders of the citadel: workers' shanties, small roadside groceries, restaurants and taverns, all blown down by the shock wave from the Gatun detonation.

Beyond that desolation was the newly widened canal, visible in spots, its rampaging waters a blur as the Jeep raced for safety. Donovan and Charlie strained to see *Liberator*, but she was nowhere to be seen. Donovan assumed Percy had turned her starboard into the lake, there to sit out the attack and await instructions.

The sound of Gital's artillery soon faded and was gone, and the only sound thereafter was that of the Jeep and silence. Nothing moved on the built-up side of the road, and the only movement in and over the swamp was birds.

Mendosa steered them to the church. Ten miles from the citadel, the road branched and branched again, the right-hand turn in both cases taking them onto an old dirt road—a cow path, really—that twisted and turned as it ran along the canal bank. They drove through a hamlet, as deserted as a ghost town and twice as unsettling. Far enough from the Gatun blast to withstand the shock wave without even shattered windows, the church stood eerily empty. It held no life except for two stray cats and a junkyard dog that lay, half-starved, on the wooden porch in front of a general store.

The church was an anomaly, made of imported granite blocks that had been fashioned into a semitropical version of a New England Episcopal church, complete with a bell tower and a small cemetery surrounded by a picket fence. Out back was a rectory and a two-car garage which, like every other building in town, was empty.

Donovan drove the Jeep into the garage and Charlie slammed the door down.

Late-afternoon light poured in a west window, through a years-old cobweb stretched over a wooden workbench used by a long-ago tenant to repair church vehicles. The tools were old and made of cast iron. A heavy vise held a vintage carburetor that someone had been working on, and one wall was decorated with old license plates that had been nailed to the wooden planking. They dated from 1927 through 2004 and were interspersed with yellowing photos of the church motor pool: a 1927 Model A tractor; 1939 Ford cabriolet with a rumble seat; 1946 Ford coupe, one of the last flat-head V8s; 1952 MG TD, red with a black interior, apparently from the second pastor's salad days; 1965

Le Mans hardtop; 1967 Cadillac Sedan de Ville; and a 1989 Toyota.

"If the pastor kept all these cars he would be a rich man today," Charlie said admiringly.

"Wealth is irrelevant," Donovan said. "We just passed up a king's ransom in hot gold. But these are pretty neat wheels, though. I wonder if the MG is around anyplace."

"British cars are nothing but heartache," Charlie said. "You want to spend the rest of your life tuning carburetors?"

Mendosa had the side door open and was out watching the sun prepare to set. "We seem to be alone here," he said. "Let's check out the church to make sure."

They followed him across the churchyard and he pushed open the vestry door. The church was small, for a congregation of perhaps 200 persons. It was poor, too, though not so poor that a few gold and silver ornaments couldn't be bought and kept on the tiny altar.

"People here don't steal from churches," Donovan observed.

"St. Michael's is a very small and insular congregation," Mendosa said.

"You worshipped here?"

"I am not religious. But one of my men told me of this place. I was here twice before, in the months following World War Three. It has not changed."

"No one is around," Charlie noted.

"It has stopped surprising me," Donovan said.

"Neutron bombs?" Mendosa asked. "I thought they were outlawed."

"We don't know what kind of bombs did this. Enhanced-radiation neutron weapons are one possibility. They would account for the absence of human life in so many places, as well as the relative lack of property damage."

"Neutron bomb research was financed by real estate interests," Charlie said.

"On the other hand, white-shirts have proved responsible for cleaning up a lot of bodies. Not on this side of the canal, though."

"So far," Charlie added.

"Wherever the people went, we will be safe here," Mendosa said.

"I'll try to reach the ship," Donovan said.

He took out his transceiver and brought it to his lips. "Donovan to *Liberator*, do you copy?"

There was no response.

"Donovan to *Liberator*, are you listening, Percy?"

Still nothing.

"This is a damned uncomfortable feeling," Donovan said.

"No shit," Charlie agreed. "I'd feel a whole lot better sitting on the deck right now. In any kind of weather. Try again."

"Donovan to *Liberator*, please respond." He listened a moment. "Nothing. Nada."

"Maybe we should get some altitude," Charlie suggested. "How do we get up in the bell tower?"

"This way."

Mendosa led them behind the altar to the circular stairs that led up three flights to the belfry.

The wooden steps creaked as Donovan moved slowly up them, feeling more and more like a character in an old movie. He was in a church. He felt maybe he should pray for salvation. If the ship didn't respond, he would have plenty of time and quite a good reason for prayer.

The door to the belfry was old and the cracks between the boards were a half inch wide. The rusted metal latch squeaked when Donovan pressed it, and when he pushed open the door he was met with a cobweb in the face. A swirling cloud of bats flew up and out into the approaching darkness. Donovan recoiled against them, shielding his face with his forearm.

"I hate bats," he said.

The belfry stunk of bat droppings and mold. Donovan was sure that there was no smell quite so bad as bat droppings in a humid climate. He leaned as far out into the fresh air as he could and tried again to contact the ship. After three unsuccessful tries, he gave up.

"They must be submerged," he said.

"Or dead," Charlie added.

"Don't be ridiculous. They're in Gatun Lake and submerged. No other explanation is possible."

"The sun is going down," Mendosa observed. "That is not good."

"Why? What goes on here at nights that we should worry about?"

"Jaguars. they hunt at night."

Charlie said, "We already met two of the beasts. I ain't in the mood for more."

"We may not have a choice. After sundown, the jaguars make the rules."

Baltimore Jack's house was set on the south side of the base of the volcano. It was far enough up the slope to have a stunning view of the South Pacific. A redwood deck clung to the mountainside among the trees.

After radioing their location to the other colonists in the settlement, Alex and Jennings took showers, which were both hot and satisfying. As good as conditions were on *Liberator*, the showers were never as good as they were at home. The bunks weren't as soft or as big as real beds. And there was never a chance to relax in a hammock and watch a glorious sunset.

Jack fed them fruit, vegetables, rice and fish, and gave them a tour of his house and its environs. It was quite a layout: a Swiss-style A-frame chalet with huge windows that opened onto the deck; a freshwater spring that flowed sweeter than the best imported mineral water; and a solar energy system with windmill backup that promised enough power to run such modest household needs as lights, a long-range radio, and a microwave.

The man had put a lot of effort into creating an environment compatible with his South Sea island setting. He recycled everything and abused nothing, and had in his year on Espiritu developed an extraordinary knowledge of how things work in Paradise. After a very short talk with him, though, Alex realized that Jack was missing human company and would welcome them. Moreover, he would be useful. In addition to his great knowledge there was his great strength. Baltimore Jack was a gentle giant who seemed willing to take them in as friends and neighbors.

Relaxing in the hammock with Jack and Jennings sitting nearby on deck chairs, Alex watched the stars grow in brilliance in the southern sky. "This is some place you have here," she said. "It's really wonderful."

"It sure beats rush hour traffic," Jack agreed.

"Are you sure you want to share it?"

"Yeah, I'm sure. I been alone for a year. For most of that time I wanted to be alone forever. But in the past month or two I've missed company. And like I told you on the beach, I'm not afraid anymore. Welcome to Espiritu."

"Thanks. We're both very grateful. We didn't really want to move on to another island."

"This one has got everything you need. There's more fish in the lagoon than you will ever need. And while these waters are full of sharks, they never come close enough to shore to prevent you from swimming."

"We just have to set up a workable community on the edge of the lagoon. I should be able to figure out how to improve the huts, build sanitation facilities, and so on. But I have a real problem—sixty-seven tenderfeet with no experience living in the wild. This is like teaching a bunch of grandmothers how to shoot the rapids in birchbark canoes."

"Hey . . . no sweat. A year ago I didn't know squat about living in the jungle. It comes real fast. And I can give your people pointers."

"That's great," Jennings said.

Jack turned to him, and said, "Alex is the scientist, right? And you do what?"

"Communications."

"As in radio?"

"Yeah, and sonar, lasers . . . you name it."

"There ain't much use for a laser specialist here, I got to tell you."

"I plan to spend most of my time with *Liberator*," Jennings said. "Eventually I'll settle down here. I'm a pretty good writer. Maybe I'll start a novel."

"Hey, you can do my life story," Jack said with a laugh.

"Maybe. Although my hope is to write the story of *Liberator*."

"No shit. Well, I got an old typewriter if you want to borrow it."

"I may take you up on that some day," Jennings said.

Jack stretched his arms and yawned. "So, where did you say your boyfriend is?"

"On his way to New York to rescue survivors. He should be through the Panama Canal by now."

"That's some job he cut out for himself. I'm looking forward to meeting the man."

"He'll be fascinated with *you*. And you'll like his kid brother, Charlie. Not only is he a world-class shot, he has an almost psychic ability to guess what's going to happen in the wild."

"I can understand that. When you live with animals, you kind of know what they're thinking. I have gotten to understand every sound in the jungle."

At that moment there came a howl, the same frightening howl that Alex and Jennings heard the night before.

"Except that one," Jack said.

To Donovan, the smell of bat droppings seemed to be the least of his troubles. It was sufficiently enough a pain in the ass to get him to leave the belfry, but not before scanning the horizon for movement. His eyes revealed nothing; without the night vision equipment aboard the ship they were nearly blind. Gital's army would have such gear, and the jaguars didn't need it. Donovan and his two companions might just as well have been blind.

At night, the church was black as sin. Only the several gold ornaments on the altar glistened in the starlight, and in the absolute silence every slight sound was amplified.

The moon was just rising in the east, and its light began to filter through the modest stained-glass window that was built into the east wall to take advantage of early Sunday morning sun. The colored panes of the window depicted a madonna and child surrounded by lambs and little children, with angels wafting through a powder blue sky.

Mendosa checked the two front doors to assure himself they were locked. Then he joined Donovan and Charlie in the front pew, where the increasing light from the moon gave a semblance of visibility.

"The doors are locked. We should be safe here until it is time to go to the ship."

"Where are we in relation to the canal?" Donovan asked.

"About a mile inland. A path goes through the cemetery and down to the water's edge. I don't know the way that well, but we should be able to see it in the moonlight. How will we get to the ship?"

"By inflatable boat. *Liberator* can't come to shore to pick us up, but the boats are fast and stable."

Donovan tried again to raise the ship, but again there was no response.

"I hope nothing went wrong," he said.

"I got a bad feeling about this," Charlie said.

"About the ship?"

"No, I believe in the ship. It's churches that make me nervous."

"You sound like Dad."

"Well, one damn near killed him."

"A church tried to kill your father?" Mendosa asked.

"That's how he put it. He was a policeman working on a case in New York City, and it involved the cathedral. He hadn't been to church since he was a little kid and distrusted them. Well, Mom finally talked him into marrying her in the church, and the first thing that happened when he knelt down to pray was that some lunatic tried to kill him."

"Really pissed the old boy off," Donovan said.

"So that was his last time in church. And, come to think of it, it was an Episcopal church, just like this one."

Charlie wandered up to the altar, thought for a moment of kneeling or bowing or whatever you do, and spent a few minutes eyeballing the various implements and decorations. Then he walked down the main aisle to the front doors and peeked through a crack at the outdoors.

Something was wrong. It was tingling his skin and bones, and he strained to see through the crack.

That was no good, so he unlatched the door and pushed it open a few inches. The moon was up more, its light hitting the tops of the tombstones in the cemetery. There was absolutely no motion outside, and not so much as the hint of a breeze. The air was as dead as the human population, and not even the crickets were making noise.

Charlie stepped out into the night, holding the Franchi in front of him. He had never hunted jaguars, and only recently had the experience of being hunted by them. But he knew the feeling, the tingle of blood that filled the air whenever a hunt was on. The tingle was there that night.

"Where are you going?" Donovan called.

"Out."

"Be careful."

"Yo, brother."

The air had cooled off remarkably with the fall of night, and the grass was crisp to the touch and the leaves crackled when he walked on them. Once again the stillness of the air amplified sounds; he thought he heard a faraway wailing, like a child's cry, but he couldn't be sure and anyway it disappeared after a moment.

The cemetery gate was wrought iron that had been recently painted black. And the hinges were oiled. Unlike the doors in the church and the garage, the hinges didn't squeak. Odd, taking better care of the cemetery than anything else, he thought. Then he caught himself. Stop playing detective, he thought. Just like your father.

The moon was up far enough by then to cast a light all the way to the bases of the tombstones. Charlie read the inscriptions. The earliest grave was dug in 1817; the most recent in 2000. Funny to oil the gate on a cemetery that hadn't had a customer in nine years. The people around here must have been particular about death, he thought.

In the center of the graveyard stood a large mausoleum, about ten feet wide by twenty feet long and seven feet high. Atop it was a Byzantine cross and, on a brass nameplate by the iron door, a plaque that read "A. Mendes, 1960–1990."

The moonlight touched the three stone steps that led down to the door. On one of them, glistening in the moonlight, was a muddy footprint left on the otherwise-clean stone step.

"It don't rain in Panama anymore, right?" Charlie muttered.

It was then that the massive iron door swung open without so much as a squeak. Then a huge pair of arms reached out, grabbed Charlie by the lapels, and pulled him off his feet and into the mausoleum. The door closed silently behind.

Alex said, "We heard that howl, too. Last night. It went on for hours. In fact, that was the reason we came into the jungle."

"It sounds like timber wolves," Jennings offered. "Of course, I know that's ridiculous."

"I thought it was Siberian tigers, but figured that was only my guilty conscience," Jack said.

The howling increased in volume and got nearer, and after a few minutes seemed to come from both sides of the volcano, the same as the night before.

"What the hell *is* that?" Alex asked. "No indigenous animals make that kind of noise."

"Are you sure all the natives left?"

"Every last one. You guys are the first humans I've seen in a long time. For a while I thought that howling was the wind. But it happens almost every night, whether or not there's any wind."

"*Almost* every night?" Alex asked.

"Sometimes I don't hear it for weeks. Other times it won't go away. Sometimes it's real close up. I've gone chasing it, but never found anything. It always goes away before dawn, and in the morning I'm alone and still alive."

"Are there any signs where you last heard it? Broken twigs? Footprints?"

"Nothing."

The howling changed in pitch, got deeper. The howling from the east got deeper and came closer, and the howling from the west went up in pitch and stayed the same distance away. Alex thought that both of them sounded slightly elevated, as if they were coming from the slopes of the volcano.

"Maybe it's the wailing of a restless soul," Jennings said, and earned himself two dirty looks.

The cobwebs that someone had stretched over Charlie's eyes were too thick to see through, at first. He could only see patterns of light, some dark and a few brighter, moving around slowly.

He could hear vague sounds that resolved into voices, both male and female. Within a few minutes the cobwebs parted and there came an aching in his head where it had impacted with the side of a stone coffin.

There was light in the room, and the smell of candle wax. He opened his eyes.

"Where am I? Jesus."

"He can't help you here," a woman said.

Charlie was lying on a faded surplus U.S. Army cot that had been set up in the mausoleum right next to the stone coffin. Sitting on the coffin lid, looking down at him, was a blonde in her mid-twenties with curly hair and no makeup, wearing Army fatigues and basketball sneakers. Behind her, with his arms folded, stood the man who dragged Charlie into the tomb—a towering man with a swarthy complexion and a Fu Manchu mustache.

"Did you get the license number of the truck?" Charlie asked, rubbing his head and raising himself up on his elbows.

"What truck?"

"The one that hit me."

"Nobody hit you. Hector dragged you into the tomb and you slipped."

"Excuse me for not appreciating the distinction," Charlie said. "Who are you and why did *Hector* drag me into a tomb?"

"*Who* are *you*?" she asked.

"Charlie Donovan, Chief Gunnery Officer, U.S.S. *Liberator*. We come to serve."

"What is the *Liberator*? A warship?"

"A submarine."

"Like I said, a warship."

"Not anymore. There are no wars left to fight. We're traveling the globe, helping survivors of World War Three. So which are you, survivor or white-shirt?"

"What are white-shirts?" she asked.

"The crazies on the other side of the canal. Certainly you know them. You're living in a cemetery."

"We're living in a cemetery because it's the only place we're safe," she said, rather defensively.

"Do you have a name?" Charlie asked.

"Anna."

"Who are you?"

"Survivors of Panama City and the villages along the canal," she said. "There are ten of us here."

"Ten in this tomb?"

She gestured for him to sit up and look around. "Ten in this complex. There are others like it."

The candlelit room with the coffin in the middle was, indeed, home to a tunnel that led down ten feet into darkness.

A boy of about thirteen peered warily from the tunnel entrance, his eyes fixed on Charlie.

Anna gestured. "It runs from the basement of the church, under the cemetery, and to a culvert that empties into the canal. This complex was built by the congregation to ensure the safety of the clergy during the 1998 persecution of the churches," Anna said. "It is for escape. Since it is little-known outside the congregation, it is also for safety. We live in here by day and move only by night, when the only danger is from jaguars."

"How long have you been down here?"

"Since the war. Three months or so. There is another complex like this ten miles down the road. But we have not heard from them in weeks."

"You *live* in here?"

"No one has thought to come looking for us," Anna replied.

"I don't understand just who you're hiding from? The white-shirts are across the water."

"Maybe the worst ones are. But the ones on this side of the canal are almost as bad. Worse, if you consider that they sometimes behave like normal people."

"Patino and Gital," Charlie said.

"The two leaders of the armies from the south," she said. "Yes, they are among the ones we fear. They and their fifth-columnists are treacherous. They persuade you to believe in them, and then they kill you. Who knows what they want? They kill you in the end."

"So they represent a milder form of radiation psychosis," Charlie mused. "I thought there was something wrong with those two."

"Madmen with the illusion of normalcy are the worst," Anna said.

"Gital is still out there, looking for us."

"Then that is why you took refuge in the church? Your plight is understandable. Gital and his spies are everywhere."

Charlie swung his feet off the cot and sat up. "Does this guy talk?" he asked, indicating the giant.

"Hector does not speak. His tongue was cut out by one of Gital's spies who convinced us he was a friend. Now he hides in the tunnel, awaiting the moment of his revenge."

"May revenge come swiftly and soon," Charlie swore, standing.

He peered down into the tunnel, causing the teen-aged boy to scoot away in fear. Shuffling feet told him that several others lingered down there, in dark broken only by occasional candles.

"Who are the others with you?" Anna asked.

"My brother Tom, the captain of *Liberator*. And one

of Romanus's men who defected and joined us, Colonel Mendosa."

"You say that your mission is to rescue survivors of the war. But you were soldiers in the war, no?"

"No. We were under the Arctic ice when it happened. *Liberator* had nothing to do with the war. It was started—as far as we can reconstruct events—by the Germans and finished by the Russians and Americans. But we didn't learn about it until recently. In fact, we missed the whole thing."

"And why are you in Panama?"

"We're en route to the Atlantic to rescue survivors of the war in New York. We located them by radio. But we're having trouble breaking through. The bomb that exploded over Gatun kind of spoiled things. Officers of the ship are working on the problem."

"Where is *Liberator* now?"

"I don't know. Probably in Gatun Lake, submerged. She was fired on by Gital and moved off, stranding us here."

"So you are no better off than us."

"For the time being, no. But we can leave eventually. You want to come along?"

"Our portion is to fight Patino, Gital, and Romanus, and all like them. And to rebuild our world."

"You will die if you stay here," Charlie said. "The land is radioactive and will stay that way for years and years."

"The cities are radioactive. Not so the countryside. There are scientists among us."

"Are you the leader?"

"I am the leader of this group, that is all. We are very democratic. Now, how can I help you?"

"Can you get rid of Gital for us? Patino took care of Romanus, and we took care of him. So there's only Gital left, and like I said he's looking for us."

"We can't attack him now," Anna said. "He is too strong for any one complex to attack. In time we will kill him. For now it is enough to survive. I will help you get back to your brother, and with him you will return to your ship. Your mission is important and must be continued. I will get you your gun."

Donovan said, "Didn't I warn him to be careful?"
"Who? Your brother?"
"Who else? Take a look out the door and see if you can spot him, okay? I'll try again to raise the ship."

Mendosa went to the church door, and Donovan again used his transceiver, this time with the scrambler on. "Donovan to *Liberator*, do you copy?"

"*Liberator* here, captain. This is Percy."

"It's good to hear from you Mr. Percy. What is your status?"

"We are on the surface in Gatun Lake, Captain. I thought it best to dive for a while just in case Gital has people on the shore looking for us."

"Have you seen any?"

"Negative along the lake. His only artillery is on the canal. I can report, though, that he has taken charge of Ciudad Romanus and his artillery now commands the canal."

"Can you get by him?"

"Not without risk. Captain, I can lay a missile on top of him."

"Negative. We can't afford to use them up. We may need more than one to blow the dam."

"The computer indicates that one 97N at ground level will break the dam," Percy reported.

"What about the current afterwards?"

"That's the problem, Captain. Computer says that the current will be a minimum of twenty knots and highly unstable for the immediate future. The recommendation is that we postpone our attempt to break into the Atlantic by at least several weeks, to give erosion time to widen the canal so the current can stabilize."

"Understood, Mr. Percy. Will you be able to blow the dam from your current location and then pick us up on the way back to the Pacific?"

"Negative on that. The current will be too wild to

launch boats. And we don't know exactly where you are. Where are you?"

Donovan said, "We are in a church, St. Michael's, on the road between Panama City and Ciudad Romanus. Gital's men are looking for us."

"Hold a minute and I'll call that up on the topography computer."

Donovan saw Mendosa returning from the door, and said, "Where's my brother?"

"Gone for a walk, I guess. I can't see him."

"Go out and take a look, would you? He doesn't know the lay of the land."

"The jaguars make the rules after dark, Captain," Mendosa said.

"Take a quick look just the same," Donovan said.

Percy said, "I have you on the topography monitor, Captain. Reading the church, a cemetery, some outbuildings, and a path that leads down to the old canal. There's also a culvert that drains the local roads."

"That's us. Keep listening on this frequency and I'll tell you when and where I want to be picked up. I have to go see what happened to my brother."

Alex listened to the howling as the sounds migrated along the southern rim of the volcano, seeming at various times to come from different elevations.

"I swear that noise is walking around," she said at last.

"I've tried everything to locate it," Jack said. "I triangulated on it. I went looking for it. It's never where I thought it should be. Sometimes I think it's the volcano gods."

"Volcano gods?" Jennings asked.

"That's who the natives built the *marae* to," he went on. "I mean, their forefathers built the altars. The natives I dealt with knew mainly from real estate and property values. But at some point in this island's history, the natives believed in volcano gods."

"Altars imply sacrifices," Alex said.

"Oh, very comforting," Jennings said.

"Well, that's what altars *are*. Places for sacrifices. You have to know the truth."

"Why?"

Jack continued, saying, "I didn't try a sacrifice. Maybe that would work."

"Not tonight, please," Jennings said. "Let's sleep on it."

The howling stabilized at two points on the rim of the volcano, one to the east and the other to the west of the house. After a few minutes more, the sounds quieted down a little and came less often.

"They do that," Jack said. "They come late at night and move around for a while, then they settle in until about an hour before dawn. Then they go away. Let's get some shut-eye."

"How can you sleep with that racket going on?" Jennings asked.

"It's just noise, nothing to be frightened of."

"So far," Alex said.

"I thought you were looking for Charlie," Donovan said, after finding Mendosa loitering by the door.

"I went to the road and back. He's not there. I came back to get you."

"Where the hell has he gone?"

"He's your brother. Where is he likely to go?"

"Anyplace that fancy strikes," Donovan said, taking out his Colt. "Let's stick together and take a walk."

"Remember what I said about jaguars," Mendosa said.

"You look out for the jaguars. I'll look out for Gital."

They prowled across the churchyard in the direction of the parish house, a small wood-frame home of two stories, including a slate roof. No lights were on, of course, but the moon illuminated the roof and two walls. A ten-speed bicycle stood propped up against a propane gas tank.

They circled the house, pausing to make sure that the doors were locked, then went back past the garage, checking inside with no luck. The path down to the canal was next. Donovan started down it, then noticed that the tall grass growing on the once-heavily traveled path was undisturbed. He turned away and led Mendosa to the cemetery, entering the old graveyard through a broken-down section of fence on the forest side.

The tombstones stood out like gleaming teeth in the moonlight.

"Our father had a professional fascination with corpses," Donovan said. "In the course of his life, he made quite a few himself."

"If your brother came here, I do not see him."

They walked down one aisle, looking with idle curiosity at the inscriptions, then returned by way of the other aisle.

"Nice graves," Donovan noted. "Rather well tended, considering there's no one left to do the work."

"Perhaps the dead rise to do their own housekeeping," Mendosa suggested with a faint smile.

In the bright moonlight they were standing and walking about, and against the backdrop of tombstones were as visible as lighthouses at dusk. A burst of shots rang out and marble chips flew from a nearby headstone.

"Get down!" Donovan shouted, and hit the dirt.

"What was that?" Mendosa asked.

"Gital! How did he find us so soon?"

Mendosa lifted his head and took a quick look. He brought his head back down when another several bullets blasted the stone above him.

"Two trucks on the road!" he warned.

Donovan lifted up, fired two shots at the lead truck, then dashed ten yards down the aisle and dived behind the centrally located mausoleum. After the return fire died down, Mendosa joined him.

"I saw twenty men," he reported.

"Who has time to count?" Donovan asked, putting the Colt away and unstrapping his Franchi. "Go down to the right end of this thing and fire a few shots at them. Let me get a better look."

Mendosa did as he was told, and Donovan ducked around the corner, spotted three men jogging head-down across the field that lay between the road and the cemetery, and fired on them. Two went down, hollering in pain. The third took two more steps before diving to the grass.

"Eighteen," Donovan said.

"Very good," Mendosa replied, stepping out himself and firing a few shots at a grove of trees that sheltered more soldiers. No one was hit, but heads went down.

Donovan bolted from behind the mausoleum and ran

a few yards to the east, ducking behind a particularly large marble headstone.

From there, and while still undiscovered, he saw what he was up against. The trucks were lightly armored troop carriers capable of holding twenty men each. They had somehow arrived unnoticed, perhaps by shutting off their engines and coasting the final hundred yards. But doing that implied knowledge that the church was the hiding place. How did they know?

Of the men who came in the trucks, at least ten were hiding in the grove of trees that stood near the spot where the church driveway met the coast road. Three others were down in the grass, two of them seriously injured. Mendosa said that there were twenty in all. That left seven unaccounted for.

Donovan yelled, "Mendosa! Circle around to the right of that grove. Let's get better angles on them."

And he sprinted off to the left, vaulting the cemetery fence as a dozen bullets ripped up the wood fencing behind him.

The fire came from the grove. Donovan ducked down behind the church's stone portal and returned fire. His slugs tore up the trunk of a tree and were followed by a scream. An attacker stumbled into the night, clutching at a wound that spurted blood from his side.

From the other side of the cemetery, Mendosa opened fire. Another scream went up and a man fell backwards to the ground.

Donovan ran into the church and sprinted to the back and up the stairs to the belfry, not caring about the creaking stairs or the bats.

Looking down from the tower, he surveyed the scene. The seven other men were behind the Jeeps, making ready for an attack. They were watching Mendosa as he fired on the grove from his new position. Then they left their shelter and ran up the driveway toward the church.

Donovan leaned out of the belfry and opened fire. He emptied a magazine into them, and the carnage was incredible. The 9-mm slugs cut a swath of gore through the soldiers, shattering rib cages and exploding inside the bodies in small, deadly puffs of soft lead that lacerated internal organs and caused massive bleeding, quickly fatal.

Four were down and dying; three scurried into the graveyard, perhaps trying to get behind Mendosa, more likely just panicked.

Donovan tried his transceiver. "Captain to *Liberator*, please respond."

"*Liberator* here, Captain."

"We are under attack by Gital's men! Bring the ship into the canal and put a small arms party in a boat. Get two of the Walthers up on deck and prepare to strafe the shore on my command."

"Aye, Captain. Estimated time of arrival, twenty minutes. Can you hold out?"

"We'll have to. Get a move on, Mr. Percy."

"*Liberator* out."

The group of soldiers in the grove split up, three running back to the lead truck, two heading west, in the direction of Mendosa. Donovan leaned out and fired on them, not hitting anyone but ripping up the ground and sending them diving for cover. When they jumped back and resumed running, Donovan nailed them with four slugs, killing one outright and knocking the other out with a hip shot.

"Mendosa! Get your ass back in the church!" Donovan shouted.

Mendosa took the advice, and scurried past the graveyard and into the front door of the church as Donovan's transceiver again spoke. "Captain, I just picked up a radio message from your location. A Gital field commander just called for reinforcements, reporting many dead. Good work."

"Thanks. How far away are the reinforcements?"

"Twenty minutes, according to the reply."

"Then we just may make it. Are you on your way?"

"Full speed on the surface, Captain. Rigging ship for surface attack."

"Very good, Mr. Percy," Donovan said, then added, "Where the hell is Charlie?"

Standing on the topside bridge, First Officer Percy said, "Ahead full, Mr. Hooper. Full surface speed."

From below, Hooper replied, "Ahead full, surface running."

"Bring her up to thirty knots."

"Thirty knots, aye."

As *Liberator* increased speed, waves crashed over the arched bow and white spray cascaded up onto the bridge. The ship headed southeast out of Gatun Lake and into the channel that led back to the Pacific. As she entered the canal, the current increased, and soon the ship's apparent speed was like that of a small speedboat smashing through choppy seas.

Percy said, "Mr. Hooper, what is the status of terrain memory?"

Terrain memory was an advanced sensor-dependent system that memorized the subsea profile of the ship's every course. Since no two subsea terrains were alike, the memory of that terrain could be used to guide *Liberator* on the exact course she had taken before. In this way, going back out the canal was as simple as coming in it.

"We have a match on our inbound track," Hooper replied. "Computer is reading the exact profile we came in on. No problems as far ahead as we can see."

"Small arms party to the topside bridge," Percy ordered. "Set up one of the captured Walthers on the new mount and prepare to fire on the shore. And bring up some flares, too. We may have to shed some light on the battleground."

Chief Smith had welded a machine gun mount to the aft of the topside bridge and rigged it to swivel so that it could fire to both port and starboard—and to fore and aft, if need be. With their heavy slugs and high muzzle velocity and rate of fire, the Walthers became formidable ship-to-shore batteries. By the time *Liberator* exited Gatun Lake and entered the canal, the ultramodern submarine had been transformed into a close-in killing machine.

With all sensors functioning and night vision equipment on, the ship raced into the teeth of the current at thirty knots, looking very much like a Coast Guard cutter with a bone in her teeth. Strapped in and glaring into the spray like an old whaleship captain, Percy held tight to the spray rail and felt, for the first time, the power the captain had long known when standing up to the sea and spray.

So this is what it's like to be captain, he thought, truly feeling the strength of the ship and the power of her mission for the very first time.

He said, "Mr. Hooper, raise the captain on his frequency. Tell him that *Liberator* is fully armed and ten minutes away from rendezvous."

Charlie heard the shooting despite being in a mausoleum ten feet below a cemetery.

"I got to get out of here," he said, taking back his Franchi from Anna and checking it.

"It won't be safe in the cemetery," she replied. "You will do better to go through the tunnel to the church."

"Maybe," he said. "Show me the way."

As Hector the giant cleared the way, Charlie descended a wooden ladder and entered a large, square tunnel braced by wooden timbers. Cots were laid out along one wall and along the other was furniture scavenged from dumps—small tables, banana crates doubling as dressers and storage bins, and candles placed in tin holders.

The people of the tunnel looked at him with wide eyes set in pallid skin. They looked like concentration camp survivors, frail does hiding from an ugly world. One in five looked defiant, like Anna, or tough, like Hector. It was clear that when these people got their revenge, it would be sweet and violent.

The tunnel ran off to the left and the right, the light fading in both directions. "Where does this come out in the church?" Charlie asked.

"In the vestry," Anna said. "There is a trapdoor set in the wooden floor. Beneath the door is an old wine cellar."

"And in the other direction? The culvert?"

"The tunnel intersects the culvert halfway between the road and the canal."

"Is this culvert tall enough to stand in?"

"For you, yes. It is tough for Hector."

"St. Peter's Basilica would be tough for Hector to stand in."

"But the rest of us come and go by way of the culvert all the time."

"Lead the way to the church."

"One moment," she said, then dipped into a banana crate and produced a Smith & Wesson revolver. "This is small but it does the job."

Charlie followed her down a tunnel that soon was devoid of people, with candles placed only at far-apart intervals. The tunnel kept to an even grade for a while, then went up a slight incline. The timbers supporting the tunnel grew older and some of them had the stink of wood preservative, creosote. Once under the church the tunnel widened perceptibly and the dirt floor gave way to one on which small stones and broken seashells had been laid down.

Then they came to a boxy room with a concrete floor and a wooden roof.

"This is beneath the vestry," Anna said.

"I'll go first."

Charlie pushed the trapdoor up, struggling against the weight of the small rug that concealed it. Soon the rug was pushed to one side and the door was standing up and Charlie hoisted himself up. He pulled Anna up behind him.

The sound of firing had faded, at least for a time. Charlie looked quickly around the church, then noticed that the door leading to the belfry stood ajar.

"The man never could figure how to cover his tracks," Charlie said, and led the way upstairs.

Donovan was looking out the window and speaking to the ship on the radio when Charlie and Anna burst into the room.

"Looking for me?" Charlie asked.

Donovan turned and frowned when he saw his brother. "I found him," he reported to Percy. "Let the log show he was with a broad. Donovan out."

Charlie said, "This is Anna, the leader of the local survivors. They live in tunnels beneath the church and the cemetery."

"That makes as much sense as anything else in my life," Donovan said.

"What's happening here?" Charlie asked.

"Gital found us. There were twenty men in two trucks. Mendosa and I killed a bunch of 'em, but there are still others out there and reinforcements are on the way. If you are finished making love, I need you to make war."

"That wasn't what we were doing, but I get your point. Where do you want me?"

"We have to get out of here. The ship is coming for a rendezvous in ten minutes."

"Where?"

"There's a dock area where the path from the church meets the canal," Donovan said.

Anna spoke up, saying, "I know that dock. It is near the culvert. I can take you there."

"How, by tunnel?"

"Yeah," Charlie said. "It goes to the culvert, which is to the west of here. Anna and her people get to and from the tunnels by way of the culvert."

"How'd you get *here*?" Donovan asked.

"The same way. A tunnel exits beneath the vestry. There's a trapdoor that leads to an old wine cellar. They had a pretty good life, these priests."

"Let's get out of here. Show me this tunnel."

They went down to the vestry, where Mendosa had just come in from the outside and was looking down at the trapdoor.

"Who is she?" he asked, spotting Anna.

"A friend," Donovan said. "What's it like outside?"

"Bad. Gital's reinforcements have arrived and have all the exit routes blocked. We'll never make it to the ship."

181

"We'll see about that. Mendosa, go with Anna and Charlie."

"Where to?" Charlie asked.

"I'll hold them off here. You three go down the tunnel to the culvert and wait for my signal. When you get it, take them from behind."

"Why don't we just split and the hell with them?" Charlie asked.

"Two reasons. One is they'll find the tunnel and Anna's people. The other is they're a threat to the ship. We can't make it to *Liberator* if there are two hundred guys on shore firing at us. And the ship could be damaged."

"Good point," Mendosa conceded. "But how will you signal us?"

"Don't worry," Donovan said. "You'll see it."

Anna led the way back down into the tunnel, with Charlie and Mendosa following. When they were gone, Donovan lowered the trapdoor and replaced the rug.

He went back up to the belfry. The two trucks were still there, and a man at the lead one was talking on the radio. There were four bodies lying about.

Donovan called his ship, saying, "We will rendezvous with the rescue boat in . . ." He checked his watch. "Seven minutes."

"Aye, Captain."

"I see one of Gital's men on the radio right now. Any messages?"

"Just came in, Captain. He's asking about the reinforcements. He's just been told that they're due in two minutes."

"But not here yet."

"No, Captain . . . two minutes. Is that a problem?"

"Not anymore. Stand by the flares and await my instructions."

Donovan went back downstairs, checked the front doors to assure himself that they were locked, then went out the back and got the Jeep. He backed it out of the garage and next to the church, then took a gas can out of the back seat. Back inside the church and moving quickly, he doused the floor with gas and left a trail of it leading to the wooden stairs that led up to the belfry.

From down the road to the east, a convoy of trucks and Jeeps moved quickly in the night. Their headlights cut weird trails of light in the otherwise pitch-black countryside. They were a half mile down the road. Donovan stood by the idling Jeep, a pack of matches in one hand and the transceiver in the other.

He lit the matches and tossed the pack into the church. "Bless me father for I have sinned," he said, and made a radio call. "Captain to *Liberator* . . . fire flares!"

"Flares fired!" Percy replied, and one after another, six high-intensity magnesium flares with the combined lighting capacity of a major league ballpark shot into the Panamanian night and lit up the heavens above St. Michael's Church. At the same time, the gasoline inside the church went up in a *whoosh* of firestorm.

"Holy shit!" Mendosa exclaimed as the sky burst into fire above him.

"You took the words right out of my mouth," Charlie said, cocking both Franchis and charging down the road from the west, where the culvert met the paved road.

Mendosa started after him, then hesitated and held back. "I will wait here," he said, nearly stammering in the effort to explain himself to Anna. "There may be other men—coming from this direction."

Charlie found the original two trucks still sitting at the edge of the road near the church. The reinforcements were coming up the road from the east. Nearly everyone was looking up at the sky, where the dazzling array of flares was turning night into high noon, though some had just taken notice of the inferno blazing in the house of God.

Charlie caught two men standing by the truck's radio with his first burst, cutting both in half and dropping the pieces on the tarmac. The drivers stood by their vehicles and were the next victims. Then Charlie turned toward the men by the grove, who stood stock-still, immobilized by the light-and-sound show. Four of them remained. Two turned with weapons. Charlie sprayed them with fire, tossing their bodies back among the tree trunks.

The other two were caught from behind. Donovan came up the driveway in the Jeep, driving with one hand and firing with the other. The last two of Gital's original search party fell dying to the ground.

Charlie let out a war whoop and leaped behind the wheel of the lead truck. He started the engine, put the truck in gear, and aimed it down the road at the party of reinforcements that was chugging noisily toward them. He drove the truck a few score yards before leaping out, leaving the aimless vehicle to smash headfirst into the vanguard of the convoy. A personnel carrier turned off the road and into the shoulder, overturning and spilling hapless soldiers onto the dirt.

"Get in!" Donovan yelled, and Charlie ran to the passenger's side of his Jeep and leaped inside.

27

Percy's knuckles were white and he gripped the splash rail for dear life.

Liberator charged up the raging current like a salmon swimming upstream, throwing spray in all directions and now calling attention to herself by shooting flares into the pitch-black night.

To starboard, the bonfires of the white-shirts blazed on. The bastards never seemed to run out of bodies to burn. To port, Gital had brought up two artillery pieces. They were hidden in the bushes by the side of the canal. Percy couldn't get a good look at them, even with the night vision equipment, but one looked like an old World War Two 88-mm, and the other two looked like similar-vintage 50-mm guns.

"How did Gital know we'd be moving up the canal?" Percy asked, forgetting that his mike was open.

"Sir?" Hooper asked from below.

"Never mind. Are we still on track?"

"Right on track and the terrain remains clear as far ahead as we can see."

"Good. Distance to target?"

"Four miles, sir."

"Are the boat parties ready?"

"Ready to launch on your command."

"Small arms party on deck," Percy ordered, and from below deck three men in foul-weather gear scrambled up onto the topside bridge and began manning the just-mounted Walter PB AutoStrafe.

There were two sharp, bright blasts of flame from port. The two 50-mm guns opened up and Percy ducked as two rounds whizzed overhead, to impact on the far shore. Puffs of fire and smoke appeared, then drifted away in the wind.

"We're under attack, Captain," Percy reported on the radio.

"I'll try to make it fast," Donovan replied.

The Walther opened up on the first 50-mm. Firing from a distance of 300 yards the aim was tentative, but the muzzle velocity of the Walther was extraordinary, as was the rate of fire. Slugs tore up the gun, its mount, and its crew, and sparks started tiny fires in the radiation-dried grass.

Another round whizzed by the ship, closer this time. The 88-mm had opened up, its projectile positively roaring by and impacting in the water just ahead of the ship.

"Get the big gun!" Percy shouted, and the machine gun crew changed target.

As another round roared from the 88-mm, the Walther opened up, spraying the gun and the whole area of shore around it with fire. Percy swore he heard screams, though it was clearly impossible to hear anything above the roar of combat and the pounding water. The tracers cut swaths of light around the target, setting fires and finally igniting the spare ammunition. The big gun exploded with a blast that sent the barrel pitching forward into the canal.

As the machine gun crew turned on the remaining artillery piece, Percy saw its crew abandon their posts and run. *Liberator* opened fire anyway, and soon the last of Gital's big weapons was turned to junk.

The Walther crew cheered and Percy congratulated them. He said, "Mr. Hooper, the shore batteries are dead. Reduce speed to twenty knots and get the boat crews on deck."

"Aye, sir. I'll match speed with current and keep her in place. We are approaching the target."

Percy switched his radio to the captain's frequency,

and said, "*Liberator* to Captain, do you copy?"

"We read you, Mr. Percy. What's the ship's status?"

"The shore batteries are knocked out. We are reducing speed and launching boats. Three minutes from rendezvous. Will you be on time?"

"We may be a few minutes late. Wait for us."

"Do you require help?"

"I'll let you know," Donovan said, pushing the Jeep hard and racing up the road with the remainder of Gital's troops following. With the church blazing behind them, flames now licking up the bell tower, Donovan turned off the road not far from the culvert and pulled up. Gital's men were not far behind. Mendosa stood by the culvert, staring in astonishment at the carnage they'd left behind.

"Get in the Jeep!" Donovan shouted, waving Mendosa and Anna to join them.

When they clambered into the Jeep, Donovan put the pedal to the metal and bounced along the dirt cow path that led from the paved highway to the canal. The night was again turning black, the ship's flares reaching ground and burning out, having done their job of stunning the enemy long enough to let Donovan and Charlie escape.

The cow path was deeply rutted and laced with tree roots that appeared like speed bumps to send the occupants of the Jeep bouncing wildly in their seats.

Through the black night the smell of gunfire and magnesium flares saturated the air. Off to the east, a sharp glow through the trees told them that the church was still burning. Donovan felt glad in a way; its destruction would mask the tunnel entrance and keep safe the secret of the survivors.

Anna was a curiosity to Donovan. She had the same fighting spirit he liked in Alexandra. Like her, she was the leader of a survivors group, unafraid to take up arms and lead men. He wondered if her existence signaled the existence of survivors groups in many parts of the world. For so long he'd thought that the

San Francisco group, from whom came the colonists now settling in on Espiritu, was unique. Now other survivors groups had been found in Panama, living in tunnels to escape the local tyranny, which appeared to be yet another, not quite so murderous, form of radiation psychosis.

Anna held tight to the seat of the Jeep, concentrating on holding on yet still focusing on Mendosa. She was frowning thoughtfully. Donovan wondered if she shared his growing suspicion of the man.

The trail took a hard right turn and then emptied into a broad, grassy plaza that led down to the water. The canal was very wide at that point and shallow on the south side. The area they turned into was an old farmer's meadow, meant for grazing cattle. The grass was overgrown and shaggy, and grew on a gentle slope that disappeared under the rampaging water. The dock that used to be there had been swept away by the current, which still tore chunks out of the shoreline and carried them downstream.

Donovan looked out into the canal and saw *Liberator*. It was a majestic sight. All her running lights were aglow, with twin high-intensity spotlights sweeping the shore. She was coming up on their position, moving slowly, still a quarter mile downstream.

Donovan, Charlie and Anna leaped from the Jeep. Mendosa lingered, and soon they saw why. Ten soldiers appeared on the right, against the water, blocking their path to safety. The men were Colombian, outfitted like the ones the Americans fought in the drug wars. They carried 7.62-mm AKM assault rifles, no doubt among the ones the Soviets put on military surplus sale in the years following demilitarization. With them was Gital, another small man in a big uniform with exaggerated notions of his own importance.

Charlie raised his Franchi, but the Colombians had the drop on him.

"Put down your weapons," Gital ordered in fragmented English.

"These guys always learn to shoot, but never to talk," Charlie said.

"It ain't right," Donovan agreed.

They dropped their guns onto the grass. From his vantage point in the truck, Mendosa said, "I am sorry, Captain. But Senõr Gital and I will be needing your ship."

"Why am I not surprised?" Charlie asked, eyeballing the traitor.

"Loyalty is a peculiarly American concept," Mendosa said.

"I expected something like this, Mendosa," Donovan said. "You really didn't leave the church to look for Charlie, did you? You stayed by the door and listened to my radio conversation. And I thought it a little odd that you told me that Gital's reinforcements had arrived—two minutes before they actually did."

Mendosa shrugged. "A small oversight."

Charlie said, "You're the spy that cut out Hector's tongue, aren't you?"

"That fat pig? I should have killed him."

Gital said, "We want your ship, Captain. There is nothing in Central America for us anymore. The land is dead. There are pockets of survivors, that is true. But I don't care about them. I want freedom and power, and *Liberator* can give me both."

"You'll never get it," Donovan said. "Percy will never turn her over to you."

"Then you will die."

"That fate awaits us all."

Moving quietly, *Liberator* was in position offshore, and her spotlights converged on the canal-side confrontation. Percy's amplified voice broke the stillness of the night.

"You on the shore! Put down your weapons and release the captain and his party."

"A Mexican standoff," Charlie said.

"I think not," Gital said. "I warn you. Turn over the ship or you will die."

"No deal."

"Your men cannot fire at me without hitting you."

"Then we both will die," Donovan said. "And if I have to go, I mean to go out in a blaze of glory."

He picked up his transceiver and brought it to his lips.

"Watch what you say!" Gital warned.

"Percy . . . nuke 'em!"

"What!" Gital screamed.

"Lay one right on top of us."

Gital's eyes were as big as pies as a flash of light shot up from the bridge of *Liberator* and raced overhead. Then there was a searing noise and a blinding flash of light as a magnesium flare incinerated the darkness.

Gital and his men were stunned, blinded. Charlie scooped up his Franchi and emptied the magazine into them. Ten men and their commander were cut to pieces and deposited on the grass, writhing in pain and screaming for quick death.

It was over in a second. Mendosa, horrified, leaped off the Jeep and stumbled toward the darkness and safety, only to crash right into Hector's arms. Mendosa shrieked as the giant lifted him by his neck, crushing his windpipe with a massive right hand. He tossed the lifeless body to the ground, an early breakfast for the jaguars.

"We have peace in our time," Donovan said.

Two boats left *Liberator* and approached shore, each with an armed guard standing in the bow. Anna ran to Hector and embraced him, then gave Charlie a hug.

"You have freed my people from the tyrants," she said.

"Come with us. That's no kind of life, living in tunnels."

"We can live on the surface now."

"The surface is contaminated with radiation."

"Then we will move inland to where it is safe. We cannot run away from our homeland. There is a future to build."

"You can always count on us to help," Donovan said, handing over his transceiver. "Call us on this in an emergency. We are only a week away."

"I will," she said, giving him a big, sloppy kiss on the cheek.

The boats arrived; a few minutes later, they were back on board and Anna and Hector had returned to take the good news to their people.

28

It was Donovan's first nuclear detonation. That is to say, it was the first that he launched and watched from the bridge of *Liberator*. There was that little matter in San Francisco, which he ordered but didn't launch and only got to see because it nearly happened on top of him.

Percy and he stood on the bridge alongside the weapons control team, their sun-filter goggles perched on their foreheads. They looked aft as the hatch cover that sheltered the 97N launching tube retracted and the surface-launch rack lifted hydraulically into place.

Liberator was at midstream, holding a steady ten point six knots, precisely the right speed to keep her in place despite the current. Dawn was approaching and the fire at St. Michael's had burned itself out. On the other side of the canal, the white-shirts had let their fires burn down to a minimum. In the annals of white-shirt behavior, the hours before dawn were most often a time of minimal activity. Smoke trails decorated the sky on both sides of the canal, and the air carried a mixed message of salt water and burned wood.

The details of blowing the dam had been meticulously worked out. Distance was determined to both shores and the site, and the target was selected taking into consideration the videos that Charlie had made of the dam. Considering the depth, thickness, and porosity of the structure, the warhead was set to detonate underwater at a point thirty-seven percent in from the upstream edge of the dam. The computer estimated that a precise placement would vaporize a big enough chunk of the heavy earthen structure. The water would then pour through, carrying the rest of it away.

Once the dam was blown, the current would zoom up to twenty point six knots and would be unpredictable. Until it settled down—a process that would take weeks and see more of the countryside eroded, probably including Ciudad Romanus—there would be no chance to break through into the Atlantic safely. But what they were about to do would create a permanent Strait of Panama that would facilitate *Liberator*'s passage between the world's two great oceans for years to come.

"I thought of another rationalization for what we are about to do," Donovan said.

"Oh?" Percy asked.

"The further erosion of the countryside here means that most of the irradiated soil will be carried away. The land will again be safe for Anna and her people."

"Are you sure that will happen?"

"I checked it on the computer myself."

"Let's hope it will also carry away the white-shirts on the north bank," Percy said.

"It should do that, too."

"Then let's do it," Percy said.

"Very well. Cameras on."

"Cameras on," Charlie echoed.

"Carry this on all monitors—the opening of the Strait of Panama."

"All hands are getting it."

"You may fire when ready, Percy."

He gave the word to Weapons Control, and a Mark 97N missile roared into the coming daylight. It cut a high, short trajectory, dropping nearly straight down on the target.

All hands on the bridge lowered their goggles and watched. The fireball was short and glorious. The top third of the earthen dam evaporated, and along with it several million tons of water. Fire and steam shot into the air, and there was a shock wave that rocked *Liberator* and kept the bridge crew hanging tightly to the splash rail.

As the small mushroom cloud reached skyward, Donovan gave the order to bring the speed up to more than twenty point six knots. Mr. Hooper pushed the accelerator all the way forward, and *Liberator*'s engines drove the submarine forward with all her might. As the forward speed indicator moved up past twenty, twenty-five, and thirty knots, the land shook and the canal seemed to shudder, as if a knife had been driven into its heart.

The speed of the current jerked upwards. *Liberator* smashed through the water at her top surface speed, as it was still too shallow to dive, and was going fast enough so that when the dam blew and the water rammed through the larger chasm, the ship was going fast enough to withstand the buffeting.

When the thrill of watching the detonation subsided, Donovan turned his attention forward and took off the goggles. As the ship's speed increased, the terrain flew by. Finally, he went below and with Hooper at the helm and terrain memory engaged, *Liberator* moved swiftly back out the canal the way she had come in. By the time the sun was squarely above the horizon she was once again out in the Golfo de Panamá on her way to the Pacific.

Donovan took her down to 700 feet and, sitting in his captain's chair again after the short but harrowing excursion on shore, felt drained, exhausted. He realized that as powerful as the ship was, her men were extremely vulnerable on shore. It would be important, in the years to come, to avoid thinking too much of their ship's invincibility. On shore they were just men, and as men subject to the dangers of the new world, including deranged civilians as well as newly aggressive wild animals. More than ever since the age of the dinosaurs, it truly was a jungle out there.

Donovan was tired, and his bunk beckoned.

"Course, Captain?" Hooper asked.
"Take us home, Mr. Hooper."
"Home, Captain?" the young man asked.
"Set course for Espiritu," Donovan said. "Full ahead."

Baltimore Jack served a breakfast of flapjacks and mango, complete with old decaffeinated coffee (of which he said, "It's good to avoid being too stimulated when you're living in the jungle").

"I bet Donovan's been sleeping like a baby in his soft bunk," Alex said.

"We don't know. He should be in New York by now, rescuing survivors," Jennings said. "We're not due to get a report from the ship for a few days."

Jack, Jennings, and Alex had been out for two hours prior to dawn, looking for the source of the last night's howling. They found nothing. The noise was real but the trail was as cold as a frozen cod.

"At least we worked up an appetite," Alex said.

"What will *you* do?" Jack asked. "Stick around here or go back to the settlement?"

"Go back, of course. There's lots to do, and we're new in this neck of the woods."

"I'll come along and help."

"Are you sure you have time?"

"I'm not sure. Let me check my calendar."

"We *do* need advice on water supply, local wind conditions, and fishing. Do you know how the natives set their nets?"

"I've seen it done," Jack said. "Sure . . . we'll work out something."

Alex finished her coffee and was given more. She took the cup and walked across the deck, looking out at a forest of palms, parrots and monkeys far removed from the destroyed civilization she just fled.

On the lagoon end of the island, sixty-seven colonists were in their second day of their new home. At the moment they were scrounging around for pots and pans and learning now to pick breadfruit and light campfires. Soon there would be formal procedures: where to live, bathe, swim, fish for food. How to heal cuts with native medicines; build huts that would stand up through the monsoon; and have and raise babies. Alex wondered if she would be the first of the colonists to give birth. She wasn't pregnant at that moment; there had been a time the month before when she had hoped she was and been disappointed.

But Donovan would be home soon, and there would be another chance.

Baltimore Jack carried the breakfast dishes inside the house, then emerged with a new mission. "Let's start back to the settlement," he said. "It's time for you folks to get organized."

Espiritu appeared in the early-morning fog, growing as an island of green in a clear blue sea. After the desolation of Panama, it was an emerald in the morning.

"Land ho," Donovan said, with a smile.

"And not a moment too soon," Percy agreed.

"Try to raise them, Charlie. You have Alex's frequency stored in memory."

"*Liberator* to Espiritu, do you copy?"

There was no reply. Only a trace of static broke a still silence on the airwaves.

"*Liberator* to Espiritu, please respond."

"Maybe they haven't got a transmitter set up yet," Percy suggested.

"Bullshit! It was one of the first things they were going to do. Besides, the yachts we liberated all have good transmitters. Charlie, if you don't get anything on Alex's frequency, try the marine band."

"Relax, big brother. We only just pulled into town."

Espiritu grew rapidly out of the fog, growing until it dominated the western horizon. Two small cumulus clouds, not noticeable before, hung over the tip of the volcano.

Liberator's radio spoke. "*Liberator*, this is Espiritu Control, welcome home."

"Espiritu *Control*?" Donovan said.

"I guess they had time to set up," Charlie replied, handing the mike to the captain.

He said, "Espiritu Control, this is Donovan commanding, U.S.S. *Liberator*, permission requested to land."

"Permission granted," Alex radioed back. "So, are you home from your vacation, Donovan? Things were really hairy here."

"Panama was a snap," he replied, adding a sideways wink at Percy, who shook his head.

"What can happen to a guy in Panama? Maybe trip over a banana peel. Tell me what happened in New York."

"We'll do New York next month."

"What happened?"

"There were complications in Panama. Can we discuss it later?"

"Sure thing, Donovan. Come ashore on the northeast side of the island. The boats are anchored there."

"Will you meet me?" he asked.

"With bells on my toes," she said.

Liberator swung to starboard and cruised around the entire island of Espiritu at a distance of five miles, using laser and sonar sensors to plot the sea bottom, approaches to the island, and the structure of the coral reef. These measurements were fed into terrain memory and other computer programs for future reference and for the all-important task of building a harbor in the lagoon.

Donovan found the fleet right where Alex said he would and, on the seventeenth day of the third month of her travels through the wasteland left by the war, *Liberator* dropped anchor off her new home.

The crew poured out onto the deck to take a look. For the first time in her life, no one stayed below to watch the controls. They walked up and down on deck, oohing and aahing at the patch of lush tropical vegetation floating in the crystal blue sea.

The officers went ashore in two boats. Donovan stepped onto the beach first, and got a hug and a kiss from Alex and a hearty handshake from Jennings.

"How did you manage communications without me?" he asked.

"It was rough. I'm putting my brother back on guard duty."

Donovan surveyed the colonists who had come to the beach to greet the crew and spotted Baltimore Jack, who stood head and shoulders above the rest.

"Where'd you find the mountain?" he asked Alex.

"The mountain came to Mohammed," she replied. "He found us. He owns this island."

"What do you mean 'owns'?"

"Owns as in bought it before the war."

"Private property is a troublesome concept in this circumstance," Donovan said. "Will he let us stay, or do I have to negotiate?"

"We can stay. He's a good guy, Donovan. A bit of a loner, but strong and knowledgeable about jungles. He took us wolf hunting the other night, but we didn't catch any."

"Wolf hunting?"

"A long story, one that can wait till we're alone."

"Panama is a long story, too."

"Good. We'll have plenty to do when we're alone."

"No shit," Donovan said emphatically.

Two by two, the men of *Liberator* swarmed ashore. Most rode in on the inflatables, but a few—Mr. Hooper started it—chose to strip to their skivvies and swim. Chief Smith was thrown overboard and made it to shore on his own, splashing his arms and waving.

As for the others, the next few days were for settling into their new home. The men formed friendships and alliances and renewed acquaintances formed in San Francisco. Hooper and Smith resumed their argument over who knew more technology. Jennings and Baltimore Jack embarked upon a wolf hunt that turned into a three-day marathon. Dr. Fisher worked aboard the *Liberator* with the ship's testing equipment and computer capacity to continue the search for the cure to radiation sickness.

Chief Smith had the task of building the permanent dock for *Liberator*. It replaced the initial mooring system, which was little more than an elaborate series of bow, stern, and spring lines tied to the trunks of palm trees. Completed at the end of *Liberator*'s first year at Espiritu, it was made of palm logs and cut planking brought over from Papeete tied to the afterdeck. But the crowning part of Smith's work—in the minds of the colonists—was the installation of the MicroScale Home Nuclear Unit pilfered from the late General Romanus.

Placed on a concrete platform located on the old site of the altar, the micronuke was planned to begin operation after less than a month. It would immediately serve the people's needs for power. There were rules, of course. No technology was to be introduced that created a dependency upon off-island resources. There would be no radios, other than the ones essential for communication, especially far communication with *Liberator* on her worldwide explorations and rescue missions. To that end, a powerful transmitter would be created with an antenna high up the eastern slope of the volcano. In all, the micronuke was to supply dependable power for essential needs and nobody was to hook up anything fancier than a refrigerator.

29

"So do you want to get up and go wolf hunting?" Alex asked, tracing a finger along Donovan's rib cage.

"I'll settle for breakfast in bed," he replied, playfully flicking a fingertip at a tiny and harmless land crab that had wandered into the hut and was looking for scraps of food.

They were lying on a woven-reed mat several layers thick and covered with a white bed sheet. In all the planning for the making of their new home on Espiritu, no one had thought of mattresses. They were, like toothpaste and underarm deodorant, "something we'll start worrying about tomorrow."

"Can't we take the bunks out of *Liberator* and bring them ashore?" she asked.

"Absolutely not! My men need comfort at sea. This thing is soft enough."

He illustrated his point by thumping the mattress with a closed fist. It made a sound like crunching old hay.

"This is true comfort," he added.

"Donovan, shut up and let me show you true comfort," Alex replied, stretching out her body and opening her legs wide and pulling him atop her and inside.

"I missed you," he whispered.

"Welcome home, sailor."

When they pulled apart both were soaked with sweat and the mattress no longer mattered. They lay entwined for a long time, listening to the sunrise chorus of birds that permeated every South Pacific island.

Then, before the rest of the colonists were awake and only the sentry patrol stirred, Donovan and Alex ran down the short trail to the lagoon and plunged into the tepid water. They swam out a hundred yards, then treaded water and watched the first rays of dawn as they penetrated the surface of the legendary bottomless lagoon.

Once back on shore, they dried off and paused for a moment to look at *Liberator* riding peacefully at anchor offshore. He could just make out the wild flowers someone had picked and placed in a bowl on the foredeck. *Mayflower II* was anchored closer to shore, inside the coral reef. A small child sat on the rail along the port quarter fishing with a bamboo pole.

"You'll have to sign it, you know," Alex told Donovan.

"Sign what?"

"The New Mayflower Compact, what else? On the day before *Liberator* got back from Panama, all the adults of the colony decided upon a body of rudimentary laws, mainly the rule of the majority. We all signed it, and now it's your turn."

"I'm a citizen of the world," Donovan replied. "And the captain of *Liberator*."

"You're an adult voting resident of Espiritu, and because you happen to command the most powerful force on Earth, it's especially important that you agree to be subject to our laws."

"I'm not going to be home a whole lot," he objected.

"You'll be home often enough, and when you leave I'm going with you. Besides, all members of your crew have signed. You're the only holdout. Come on, Donovan, yield to the logic of the situation."

"All right, I'll sign. Do I have to pay income taxes, too?"

"Not yet, but it may happen. The price of civilization . . ."

"Is too high," he said. "Let's go home and eat. I have a busy day ahead of me ... blasting a harbor out of that coral reef."

"The calculations have all been made," she said. "I'm sure that Jennings and I got it right. You have nothing to worry about."

"It isn't blowing a hole in the reef that worries me," Donovan said, looking far out to sea.

"What, then?"

"Never mind. Anyway, I'm hoping I'm wrong."

Liberator weighed anchor at 1100 hours, sailing, once again, with both Jennings and Alex on board. Jennings was back in his old post as communications officer, and Alex was the chief scientist and computer expert.

Sailing opposite to the direction she took on the way in, *Liberator* slowly circumnavigated the island, making observations of the thickness of the coral. Those observations were compared with ones taken the day before, and the calculations were made by the computer with Alex and Jennings keeping an eye on the proceedings. The diagnosis finally came in: a single Mark 70 torpedo set to explode forty feet down at a point on the coral precisely 457 yards north a line bisecting the lagoon on the west-east axis.

The Mark 70 had a range of 25,000 yards and was extraordinarily accurate even at that distance. But Donovan wanted pinpoint accuracy, and so decided to fire from point-blank range—1,000 yards. The torpedo had to hit a target the size of a bushel basket, but that spot was well illuminated by the forward laser, which kept its lock on the target even as Hooper turned the ship to starboard and brought her into position.

The fleet sailed along with *Liberator*, a kind of spectator fleet. They would be sailing into the lagoon in her wake, that was true. But mostly they wanted to watch the demolition, and most of the colonists returned to sea for the occasion. As *Liberator* stood out to the east of the island, her bow turned toward the lagoon, they were arrayed behind her under sail, white cotton puffs against the horizon.

The officers kept watch from the bow, with Donovan gripping the splash rail every bit as tightly as he had coming out of the Strait of Panama. It was high noon in the Society Islands. Percy said, "Weapons Control reports ready, Captain. Torpedo room is ready."

"Give the order, Mr. Percy," Donovan said.

"Fire torpedo," Percy ordered.

The Mark 70 burst from the tube amidst a cloud of condensed air and kicked to life just ahead of the bow. As Donovan and the other men and women of *Liberator* watched from the deck and on monitors, the torpedo zoomed straight and true to the target. It exploded with a deep rumble that pulverized the coral reef from top to bottom and 100 feet across and sent a shock wave of sound that vibrated through the hull of *Liberator* and far out to sea.

Cheers went up from all sides. Each of the boats in the fleet sounded her horn, and colonists waved to herald the entrance to their new harbor and home. "We did it!" Charlie exclaimed, wrapping up his brother and Alex in a gigantic bear hug.

"We sure did," Donovan replied.

Percy said, "The laser indicates we have broken through. Sonar also shows a channel one hundred feet wide and sixty feet deep."

"Send the fleet through, Mr. Percy."

The others looked at Donovan as if he were a little mad. After all, the pride of the fleet was expected to lead the fleet in. "But Captain . . ." Smith complained, and was waved silent.

Donovan said, "Get the fleet into the harbor and the crew below decks. Mr. Hooper, reverse course and take us out to sea."

"What heading, Captain?"

"It doesn't matter . . . east. Once everyone is below we'll dive to periscope depth. Once we have enough water, we'll go to four hundred feet."

"Aye, Captain, beginning our turn."

"Ahead one-quarter. Mr. Percy, we'll be going to alert stations. Full sweeps on all sensors."

Percy caught on, and said, "Are we looking for echoes, Captain?"

"Very good. We're looking for a duplicate of our own sounds. Especially cavitation and pump noises."

"*Nemesis*," Percy said.

"I did some computer work of my own, and found out that the sound we just made will be audible for two thousand miles with a typical ship's listening gear. With advanced hydrophones the noise should be audible halfway around the world."

"Noise attracts sharks," Charlie added.

"Yeah, and there are lots in these waters. More important, though, it wasn't so long ago that we chased *Nemesis* from a patch of sea not far from here."

"And she *does* have an uncanny way of finding us," Charlie said.

"She'll be looking after hearing that explosion," Donovan said. "And if she is going to find us, I want it to happen far from Espiritu."

With the crew below deck and the hatch sealed, Donovan took the ship down to periscope depth and then, a few miles farther out to sea, down to 400 feet.

"Ahead full, Mr. Hooper," Donovan said, and the ship surged forward into the deep ocean, lasers and sonar operating at peak efficiency, sweeping the sea for contacts. The Cyclops display showed it all—sharks, whales, thermoclines, and currents—even floating patches of algae stirred up by far-away storms.

"Mr. Percy, load tubes one and two, magnetic fuse, proximity targeting."

"Aye, Captain."

"The sonar is programmed to look for harmonics," Jennings said.

Alex said, "We'll get her this time. I've programmed the sound recognition system to reject everything that is an exact harmonic off us. *Nemesis* sounds like *Liberator*, but the sound isn't an exact match. It's off by twenty-seven thousandths, which is enough for us to detect her."

"Are there any conditions under which she can hide from us?"

"Yes. Running with a background of soft sediment that absorbs our sonar and lasers. But those conditions don't apply here."

"Then we have a chance," Donovan said.

"*If* she's out here looking for us," Percy said.

Liberator continued out to sea at forty knots, a modest cruising speed, for ten hours, until she was hundreds of miles from home.

"Home" was what all members of the crew called Espiritu from the moment they set foot on the island, and Donovan felt a keen sense of protectiveness about the island. If he had to fight *Nemesis* he would do it on his terms, in the deep sea, where the colonists and home would not be threatened.

At 2200 Donovan turned the ship to port and began a long sweep north in the general direction of the shipping lane that led into Papeete and beyond to New Zealand. If there was a logical place to find *Nemesis* it would be there.

"She has to be looking for us," Donovan mused as the night dragged on. "We represent the last of America to her. If she is our counterpart, built in secrecy by the Germans and then turned against us, she can't let us live. Our continued existence is the only threat to her domination of the world."

"If she was listening for low-frequency sounds and heard the harbor-building explosion," Alex said, "she probably sailed in the direction of Papeete. It's the only major city in this part of the world. The only place around here you would expect us to find anything to shoot at."

"*Nemesis* is nearby," Charlie said. "I can feel it."

30

At 0400 Donovan ordered a turn back to the west, which would take the ship home.

After steaming an hour on that heading, everyone was uneasy. Charlie was the most upset. His legendary intuition had been percolating for hours, yet nothing came up on sensors.

Every sound the ship put out came back intact. There was no problem with harmonics. Each echo was perfect, as if a sonic reflection cage was out there sending back exactly what it got.

"This ship's sonic environment is right out of the design lab," Chief Smith complained. "I been reading the monitors, and even that booster coil that went bad last month can be read through the echoes."

"You didn't tell me about a coil problem," Donovan said. "Afraid of pissing off the boss?"

"It was nothing. Just a weird electronic that put out a five-hundred-seventy-eight-hertz vibration."

"What frequency was that?" Jennings asked.

"Five hundred seventy-eight," Smith repeated.

Jennings looked at his monitors, then scratched his head. "I don't understand how we're getting back an echo on that," he said. "All frequencies from five fifty to six hundred are being absorbed by the wave boundary layer at this speed and depth."

"Meaning?" Alex said, for once a bit put off by ship technology.

"Meaning that booster coil emissions shouldn't get

more than ten feet outside the hull of the ship. We shouldn't be getting an echo because the sound isn't going far enough to bounce off anything."

"She's out there," Charlie said, the hairs on the back of his neck standing up.

"And mimicking our sound," Donovan said. "Hard a'starboard, Mr. Hooper! Give me flank speed! Jennings, read differences. See if she can keep up with our noise changes."

Liberator had been traveling at a constant speed and depth for hours and had grown easy to imitate. But as the ship turned and sped up, computers analyzed the differing echoes and soon had a target.

"I got her, Captain!" Jennings said. "Four thousand yards and off the starboard bow! We're turning into her! Damned if she isn't a pretty target!"

"On Cyclops!"

Donovan watched as the submarine icon came up on the main viewscreen, larger than before because she was so close. *Nemesis* was caught off guard by the sudden change in tactics and lay in Donovan's sights.

"She's turning to port and accelerating," Jennings reported.

"Hooper, keep turning into her. Percy, is the torpedo room ready?"

"Torpedo room is ready, Captain," Percy replied.

"Lasers from probe to weapons status. Get me a lock."

"Aye, Captain, we have a laser lock," Jennings reported. "We're tying in Cyclops with Weapons Control."

"Weapons Control indicates receipt of laser lock. Feeding in to torpedo guidance."

"Stand by those torpedoes," Donovan said.

"Torpedoes ready," was the reply.

"Cavitation noises, Captain. We're reading her screw turning. Holding on for the computer match."

"Set torpedoes to ignore acoustics—respond to the laser lock only. Proximity fuse."

"Torpedoes are ready to fire."

"Fire one!"

Liberator continued to turn on the enemy and to catch up. Caught off guard, *Nemesis* wasn't accelerating like before. She seemed almost tired. Ships that have seen too much get that way.

"She's at forty knots," Hooper said.

"Stay with her."

"Aye, Captain."

"The fish is on target and accelerating. The enemy is aware of it now and diving. The fish is turning with her. Ten seconds to impact."

"Get her," Donovan swore, urging on the torpedo. "Make our new home safe."

"Eight . . . seven . . . six . . ."

"She's up to fifty knots now," Hooper said.

"Five . . . four . . . three . . ."

As *Liberator* continued to close in on the enemy, the torpedo detonated fifty yards from the skin of *Nemesis*, shoving the boat to one side and shaking her the way a shark rips a victim.

"Got her!" Donovan shouted.

"She's hit!" Percy exclaimed.

The image on the screen became indistinct, flicked on and off and on again, then stabilized somewhat to show an enemy ship that was badly shaken. She was thrown completely off her track, nearly spun around, her forward speed almost halted.

Donovan said, "Ready on tube two! Lasers, fire!"

The blue-green lasers seared out from their ports and peppered the skin of *Nemesis*, disrupting electrical circuits and bulkhead-mounted systems. Electrical fire flickered across her dark skin, looking like fireflies in the black of the ocean depths.

"She's nose down," Hooper said, astonished, his young eyes wide as silver dollars. "Twenty degrees down by the bow. Captain, she's accelerating toward the bottom."

"Diving or sinking?" Donovan asked.

"Maybe both."

"We got her!" Charlie said. "Damned if we didn't get her!"

"She was wrong to come after us this last time," Smith said.

"Enemy is making fifty-three knots in her dive," Hooper said.

"Tube two stands ready, Captain," Percy reminded.

"Hold your fire," Donovan said, holding up his hand to make the point.

"But, Captain . . . we can finish her."

Nemesis appeared on Cyclops as a sick and dying fish hurtling toward the bottom and certain destruction. Life was certainly fleeing her, Donovan thought. Why add insult to injury with an unnecessary, final shot? Even as he thought, she was slipping out of the reach of the viewscreen, becoming tiny and distant as the abyssal depths beckoned.

"We only have a handful of these torpedoes left," Donovan reasoned.

"I'd waste one to be sure she's dead," Percy said.

Yeah, Donovan thought, put the bastards out of their misery. So what if they did start World War Three, as *Liberator*'s reconstruction of the history of the war seemed to show. Do they deserve to die an agonizing death with the life crushed out of them by deep seawater?

"Do we still have a lock for tube two?" he asked.

"Aye, Captain."

"Fire two. Let's be done with it."

"Two fired," Percy said, with a gush of satisfaction as the torpedo left the tube.

Alex stood behind Donovan and dug her fingers into his shoulders and they all watched as the torpedo swept away and down, pursuing the hapless ship.

Silence hung in the air of the bridge, broken only by the insistent beeping of a monitor. All eyes watched the Cyclops display, where the two images—torpedo and submarine, were converging. The images came together and for a second the display went blank.

Then there was a flash of ice-blue white followed by orange flames that spread across the three sides of the screen.

"Target hit," the display said laconically.

The roar that went up from *Liberator* personnel drowned out the noise Donovan imagined came from the hell he had created below. Alex hugged him and pressed kisses on his cheek, and Percy grasped his hand with uncharacteristic excitement.

"We did it, Captain! We did it!"

Donovan leaned into the display and watched. The lights of destruction were gone, replaced by sounds: of hull plates tearing, water escaping under pressure, steel beams twisting.

"Her back is broken," Donovan said quietly, acknowledging the sound of a ship's steel keel snapping in half under the hull's dripping weight.

The cheering died down and men on the bridge looked at the display to see the sight behind the sound, but there was none.

"Why can't we see this?" Percy asked Jennings, who as communications officer was responsible for the Cyclops's outside inputs.

"I have no idea. The sensors could be reflecting off the shock wave."

"What shock wave?" Donovan asked. "I don't hear anything. Are speakers on?"

"Hydrophones are operating nominally," Jennings said. "After all, we heard her break up."

"All stop," Donovan said. "Lasers from weapons to probe status. I want to see that wreck."

"But Captain, she's sinking ... halfway to the bottom now," Hooper protested.

"We can see dolphins a mile away. I want to see the pieces of that ship. We heard her break up. Show me the debris."

"All stop," Hooper replied. "Slowing to dead slow ... stopping."

"Lasers on probe status," Jennings said. "Reading the bottom. I get sediment, thick sediment, mean depth of sea beneath the keel is three thousand, four hundred fifty-one yards."

"Where's *Nemesis*?" Donovan thundered.

"Unknown, Captain. Maybe she buried herself in the sediment. We can't read through mud."

Percy said, "There is a precedent. Remember the *Thresher*? When she went down in the North Atlantic in 1963 she buried herself ninety feet in mud."

"*Thresher* sank with her hull intact," Donovan said. "We just blew *Nemesis* to shit. At least I thought we did."

"We all heard her break up," Jennings said.

"I know. The sound of a ship's back breaking, of tearing steel, is one-of-a-kind. We're all familiar with it from records of experimental ship sinkings used to program our war games simulations."

"I've heard it a million times," Percy said.

Donovan pounded a fist into a palm, and said, "Dammit! Neosteel doesn't tear! Old hulls break up like we expect them to, not new hulls like *Nemesis*'s . . . and ours!"

"What do you mean?"

"That wasn't a sinking we witnessed! That was a fuckin' sound-and-light show! Mr. Hooper, ahead flank! Emergency speed!"

"You d-don't think . . ." Percy stammered.

"I can't take the chance. Load tubes three and four."

As the ship accelerated, Jennings said, "You mean that whole thing was fake? To set us up for an easy kill?"

"We'll know soon. Sweep the horizon, Mr. Jennings. If a fish farts, I want to know about it."

"How could they fake that?" Alex asked.

"They used bioacoustic damping to mask their own noise. They can fake their own destruction by feeding us sound effects. There isn't much that that ship can't do."

"Except kill us. Donovan, I think you're overreacting."

"We'll see. Mr. Jennings, are there any contacts?"

"Nothing. Not even fish farting. It's dead out there."

"Read the bottom again. Is there any debris from the destruction of *Nemesis*?"

"Nothing," Jennings said. "Captain, in my opinion she buried herself in the mud."

"Your opinion has been noted," Donovan said icily.

Jennings said, "I'm scanning for *Nemesis*'s torpedo signature. There's nothing."

Hooper said, "Course, Captain?"

"I don't care as long as it's away from home. Confuse them."

"Confuse *who*?" Alex said. "We're all alone."

"I'll believe that when we're *left* alone, preferably forever," Donovan said. "Continue at flank speed, Mr. Hooper. Maintain alert stations. I'll tell you when to stop."

Three days and three nights passed. *Liberator* patrolled the South Pacific, circumnavigating the Society Islands and searching all nearby shipping channels.

She went southeast to the Duke of Gloucester Islands, skimming far-flung Nukutipipi before turning north to cross the channel between Ravahere and Hao. Donovan took her north to the Disappointment Islands, turning around Napuka and heading south of west to the King George Islands and Mataiva before turning south to home.

Crossing the deep water west of Makatea, Donovan brought the ship to the surface and ran slowly on top, resting his crew and, for a time, sitting in his favored spot near the bow and losing himself in recorded music. This time it was one of his father's favorites, the Grateful Dead.

Alex approached him, ruffling his hair before sitting next to him, letting the warm South Seas water lap over her ankles.

"Well, Ahab, is the quest over? We all want to go home."

"We are not amused," Donovan said.

"Come on, lover. Give up on it. You sank the enemy and the sea is now ours. Just because you can't find the body is no reason to keep on looking. *Nemesis* is dead."

"I'll admit only that I can't find her."

"She didn't fire on us after she faked her death like

you thought, the reason being that she really died. We took a vote."

"Another one?" he said with a groan.

"Yes, Donovan, another one. You signed the New Mayflower Compact agreeing to submit to the will of the majority."

"I don't believe I'm hearing this," Donovan said.

"The war is *over*. The enemy ship started World War Three and you sank her. The seas are now ours. *Liberator* is no longer a warship. There no longer is anyone to fight."

"We'll see."

"Why do you cling so doggedly to outdated notions of war and conflict? This is a new age, Donovan."

"There is no new. Only new versions of the old. Put in the vernacular, 'same shit, different day.' So, I guess the crew voted to give up the search for *Nemesis* and go home?"

"Yes. For the third time."

"And this being the new age, I have to go along."

"You don't *have* to. You *are* the captain . . ."

"Thank you for remembering that," he said sharply.

"But it's the logical thing to do," Alex added. "Besides, it sets a good example. If the rough, tough, submarine captain can yield to a majority vote, there's hope for everyone."

Donovan turned off the disk player and stood. "What a long, strange trip it's been," he said, stretching and yawning.

Alex turned and gave a thumbs-up sign to the men on the bridge, who cheered. Donovan scowled at them. "The democrats on this ship will live to regret it," he snarled.

Alex hooked her hand in his arm and steered him aft. "Let's go home," she said.

The men and women of *Liberator* went home in the fourth month of their adventures.

At noon of a gorgeous day four days after the battle with their adversary, *Liberator* sailed through the entrance to the lagoon and Donovan watched as the shark net closed behind them.

The rest of the fleet was already anchored. With *Liberator* in place at her mooring, six ships lay at anchor in the west end of the lagoon, making for a floating colony just down the trail from the onshore settlement. The micronuke was already purring away, making energy for the people of the new colony.

The settlement was building up and out, moving into the jungle without despoiling it. Baltimore Jack, the towering figure who lorded over the island like a medieval count, helped the settlers adapt to the new conditions. Soon colonists were fishing in the lagoon and diving for shellfish in the surf outside, keeping clear of the sharks and learning the timeless ways of life in the South Pacific. In time, the first baby was born. Dr. Fisher delivered it, taking time out from his research into radiation psychosis. And his two prize patients, the teenagers Jake and Lisa who were rescued from the ashes of San Francisco, continued to serve as models for hope.

Using shipboard antennas and instruments mounted on the slope of the volcano, radios continuously monitored the world, listening for survivors. Before long the group on the outskirts of New York City was heard from again, and an expedition of rescue was planned, with the ship to head back through the Strait of Panama that she helped open. Donovan's dream of *Liberator*'s mission as a ship of rescue and salvation—of liberation, in fact—came true. And it would go on for years and become the stuff of legend.

They survived Armageddon to sail the oceans of a ravaged nightmare world

OMEGA SUB 76049-5/$2.95 US/$3.50 Can
On top secret maneuvers beneath the polar ice cap, the awesome nuclear submarine U.S.S. *Liberator* surfaces to find the Earth in flames. Civilization is no more—once-great cities have been reduced to smoky piles of radioactive ash. As their last mission, the brave men of the *Liberator* must seek out survivors in the war-blackened land.

OMEGA SUB #2: COMMAND DECISION
76206-4/$2.95 US/$3.50 Can
Beneath the still waters of the South Pacific, a high-tech Soviet submarine stalks the U.S.S. *Liberator*, intent on avenging the Motherland's destruction.

OMEGA SUB #3: CITY OF FEAR
76050-9/$2.95 US/$3.50 Can
On a grim journey through the ruins of the Panama Canal, the U.S.S. *Liberator* discovers a nightmare city under siege, prowled by man-eating predators and radiation-crazed "whiteshirts."

Buy these books at your local bookstore or use this coupon for ordering:

Mail to: Avon Books, Dept BP, Box 767, Rte 2, Dresden, TN 38225
Please send me the book(s) I have checked above.
☐ My check or money order—no cash or CODs please—for $ _____ is enclosed (please add $1.00 to cover postage and handling for each book ordered to a maximum of three dollars).
☐ Charge my VISA/MC Acct# _____ Exp Date _____
Phone No _____ I am ordering a minimum of two books (please add postage and handling charge of $2.00 plus 50 cents per title after the first two books to a maximum of six dollars). For faster service, call 1-800-762-0779. Residents of Tennessee, please call 1-800-633-1607. Prices and numbers are subject to change without notice. Please allow six to eight weeks for delivery.

Name _____
Address _____
City _____ State/Zip _____

CREATED TO SERVE, NOW THEY'RE DEDICATED TO DESTROY HUMANKIND

by Mark Grant

MUTANTS AMOK   76047-9/$2.95 US/$3.50 Can

They had been bred as the perfect killing machines—vicious, fearless warriors genetically designed to triumph on the battlefields of the 21st century. But the mutant servants have revolted and a small band of human rebels—their one-time masters—are the last hope of a besieged planet.

MUTANTS AMOK #2: MUTANT HELL
76048-7/$2.95 US/$3.50 Can

An attempted revolt by a brave but foolhardy band of *Homo sapiens* guerrillas has been crushed. Their captive leader, Max Turkel, is faced with a grim and terrible choice: either slow, agonizing death at the hands of his inhuman enemies... or collaboration.

MUTANTS AMOK #3: REBEL ATTACK
76191-2/$2.95 US/$3.50 Can

The savage mutants have captured the beautiful lover of Jack Bender—leader of the courageous band of human rebels—spiriting her off to Hollywood to star in a grisly mutant "snuff" film.

Buy these books at your local bookstore or use this coupon for ordering:

Mail to: Avon Books, Dept BP, Box 767, Rte 2, Dresden, TN 38225
Please send me the book(s) I have checked above.
☐ My check or money order—no cash or CODs please—for $_____ is enclosed
(please add $1.00 to cover postage and handling for each book ordered to a maximum of three dollars).
☐ Charge my VISA/MC Acct#_____ Exp Date_____
Phone No_____ I am ordering a minimum of two books (please add postage and handling charge of $2.00 plus 50 cents per title after the first two books to a maximum of six dollars). For faster service, call 1-800-762-0779. Residents of Tennessee, please call 1-800-633-1607. Prices and numbers are subject to change without notice.
Please allow six to eight weeks for delivery.

Name_____
Address_____
City_____ State/Zip_____